SOMEONE TO WATCH OVER ME

Someone to Watch Over Me

By Taylor Michaels

Copyright 2012 by Taylor Michaels

Ebook conversion by Bella Media Management

Cover design by Char Adlesperger

First Edition

ISBN-13: 978-1480146754

SOMEONE TO WATCH OVER ME

TAYLOR MICHAELS

ABOUT THE AUTHOR

Taylor Michaels writes romantic suspense and blames it entirely on all the Nancy Drew mysteries she read as a child. A marketing professional elbow deep in reports and campaigns by day, she spends many nights writing stores where love blooms amidst danger and uncertainty. A long-time reader of romance books and thrillers, she loves the "oh my gosh, I didn't see that coming" plot twist almost as much as the happily-ever-after ending.

For more information please go to www.taylormichaels.com. In addition to author updates, she blogs about all things related to romance novels and recommends a fabulous read of the week.

CHAPTER 1

"Honey, I'm home." Morgan sang the phrase out as she locked the jewelry store's heavy metal door behind her and punched in the key code which reactivated the alarm in the retail area.

Her gaze fell to the dust-covered tables where she designed and crafted jewelry. Something she hadn't had time for in months. She stepped around them as she went to the paneled office which had been her father's until a few months ago. A virtual Mount Everest of unopened mail sat dead center in the middle of the dark mahogany desk. She took a sip from her Starbucks mocha latte and savored the rich flavor. *Just as I expected.*

For a moment, the urge to turn and flee flitted through Morgan's mind. Her chest tightened as she realized the workload of managing the store never let up. She tamped down the feeling, walked in and sank down in the large leather chair. The message light on the phone blinked to her left. She pulled out a legal pad and pen before punching the button.

"Morgan, this is Suzie. Hope the New York trip went without a hitch. Don't forget about the KDEZ interview tomorrow. I'd suggest you arrive at the station early. Please call me to confirm."

Morgan made a note, and the next message came up. "Ms. Kennedy. This is Ellen at Copper Creek Resort. I'm calling to confirm the scheduled walk through for tomorrow at 1 p.m." Morgan scribbled the number down and waited for the next phone message. The phone clicked and no one spoke. Fifteen to twenty seconds later, the caller disconnected. Morgan hit the delete button.

The next voice mail came up. Again, silence. She erased the second one. The next three calls repeated the same pattern. *What's wrong with this person?*

The computer voice introduced the next call. Morgan tightened the grip on her pen in anticipation only to have the mailbox cut off after a few seconds. She reached for her coffee and took a sip. "Whoever you are you're starting to piss me off." She murmured.

The next batch of voice messages were the same. The mystery caller dialed in frenzied bursts, and then stopped for an hour or two only to start again, never leaving a message.

"This is ridiculous," Morgan muttered. She eyed the mail in front of her and reached over and started to sift through the envelopes, pausing every few seconds to punch delete. Ten minutes later she managed to clear her voice mailbox and dump the junk mail into the waste basket.

"Dad, how did you manage?" she whispered as she stacked the invoices for the bookkeeper. Morgan took another couple sips of her coffee as she turned on the computer and brought up the company email.

The phone rang, and Morgan picked up the handset. "Kennedy's Fine Jewelry."

No one answered. Morgan couldn't be sure, but she thought she caught the sound of faint breathing. "Hello? Can I help you?"

The silence on the other end continued, and she glanced over at the number on the console of her office phone. The four eight zero area code meant the call came from the East Valley. Morgan reached for her legal pad and scribbled the number down. "I don't know who you are, but I think you have the wrong number."

"Morgan?" The deep masculine voice sounded surprised and excited. "You're at the store."

Morgan gulped. Her eyes skimmed the empty workshop area and then looked back at the alarm status. The motion detectors showed no activity on the retail area of the store. Despite being safe behind lock and key, a chill fingered its way down her spine. She was alone, and this man knew it. "Who are you and why are you calling me?"

He didn't answer. Her stomach knotted, and the coffee she sipped moments before began to burn like battery acid as the image of a faceless man on the end of the line jacking off materialized in her mind. She reached to punch the disconnect button.

"Don't leave me again."

Morgan froze. *Leave him?* This guy sounded too weird to be real. Was she being punked? She played with the pen in her hands and stared down at the phone number. *Okay mister, time to stop this game.* She squared her shoulders and took a deep breath. "Look. I've written down your number. Don't call again or I'll notify the police."

Morgan waited for a reply and prayed he'd hang up and slink back to whatever corner he'd crawled out of. The caller remained silent. "Do you understand?" she snapped.

"Don't do this again," he growled.

Morgan paused. His anger surprised her, and she tamped down her instinct to soften her approach. This man needed to learn a lesson.

"Watch me." Morgan slammed the handset down. Who did this person think he was? She didn't deserve this kind of harassment, especially now with so many things on her plate. If she could find out who her mystery man was, she'd turn the tables around on him. A visit from the police would make him understand.

Morgan glanced over at the notepad and the phone number that she'd written down. Frustration faded as curiosity took over. What would she find if she did a reverse phone look-up?

She sat back in her leather office chair forty-five minutes later and raked her hand through her hair. Playing detective had been an exercise in futility. No matter which website she used, the result was the same, nothing.

So much for coming in early to the office to get some of the paperwork done; the sales staff would be here any moment. As if on cue, the alarm went off with a high pitch monotone warning. Someone had opened the front door. Morgan listened as a series of staccato beeps followed. The security code to deactivate the alarm had been punched in. Morgan slid her chair back and walked over to the steel door which opened to the retail area of the store. She glanced through the peep hole and spied Mary. She opened the door. "Good morning."

The middle-aged lady glanced over after relocking the front door and smiled. "Hi. You're here early. Is Sarah here yet?"

"No."

Mary ambled toward Morgan after picking up her purse and lunch container. "Good. I wanted to talk with you about co-hosting a baby shower for Sarah. Sarah will be due in a few weeks, and she could still use some items."

Morgan fought the urge to wince. She'd planned to hold a baby shower when Sarah announced her pregnancy five months ago, but lately fate seemed to have conspired against her. Since her father's heart attack and by-pass surgery, she'd taken on the management of the family jewelry store. Now with the upcoming charity fundraiser, the baby shower plans had slipped through the cracks again. Morgan forced a smile. "That's a great idea. I'll host it at my house."

Mary nodded. "I hoped you would volunteer your place. I've compiled a list of people we should invite, but we need to come up with a date and run it by Sarah. "

Morgan pulled the back office door wider so the saleswoman could enter. "Mary, what would I do without you?"

The woman walked over to the refrigerator and placed her lunch inside. "You would have managed." She cracked a quick grin and added, "But it's nice to hear I'm appreciated every now and then."

"Does Sarah know if she's having a boy or girl?"

"Girl," Mary replied.

Morgan bent over, entered the combination and opened the safe. "How did Bill handle the news?"

"Sarah's husband was an outdoorsman. When she first became pregnant he had talked about teaching his son hunting and fishing, but he came around. Now he's talking about teaching his daughter when the time comes."

Morgan chuckled. "How many people are on your list?"

"I have fifteen. Just a few close friends and family. Is that okay?"

Morgan opened the door wider so Mary could reach in and pull out the first tray of jewelry. "That's fine. In fact, if we have a few extra people, I can squeeze them in."

Mary pulled the tray which held the fundraiser items and handed it to Morgan. "Here, you set up the display for this one."

Morgan glanced at the jewelry. An elegant diamond necklace and a sapphire ring with matching earrings were spread out in the tray. The Ceylon sapphires were a vibrant shade of cornflower blue, and for a fleeting moment an image of her brother Samuel pinged through her thoughts. *His eyes were blue.* If he were alive today, he'd be here as the store manager instead of me.

Mary handed another couple trays to Morgan and then she pulled another three for herself. The pair walked to the retail area. "When do you want to schedule the shower?"

Morgan's attention snapped back to the older woman. "Would a month from now work? I definitely want to get past the fundraiser so we can give Sarah's party the attention she deserves."

Mary nodded. "That's fine. That still gives us about a month before Sarah is due. I wouldn't suggest holding it any later. Who knows, this baby may decide to come early."

The pair opened separate cases and began to display the jewelry when the phone rang. Morgan jerked around. *Is it him?*

She glanced around and caught Mary looking at her with a puzzled expression. Morgan took a quick breath and grinned. "Surprised me."

For a second, she considered asking Mary to answer the call, but the little voice inside chided her to get a grip on things. Morgan slowly set the diamond rings down and answered the phone. "Kennedy's Jewelry, can I help you?"

The caller hung up, and her stomach knotted. *Oh, God. Not again.* She turned and looked out the front window of the store. *Is he out there right now watching us?*

"Showers are a lot of fun," Mary said.

"What?" Morgan looked over and watched as the mature woman finished positioning the bracelets.

"Showers, whether baby or wedding, are fun."

Morgan pressed her lips together and pretended she'd not picked up on the subtle hint her employee had made. She leaned over and started to arrange the engagement rings. "I suppose."

The woman continued. "Perhaps we'll be having a wedding shower for you soon."

Morgan swallowed and her fingers paused over a diamond ring she'd placed on a velvet display fixture before pulling back. "I don't think so. Brad and I have decided to take a bit of a break." She cast a glance over at Mary and found the woman staring at her.

"What's wrong? Isn't he ready to settle down yet?"

"What makes you think it's him? Maybe I'm the one who isn't ready." Morgan said.

"Dear, I see you when people come in the store with their children. You always ask to hold the babies and give a piece of candy to the kids. I think you'd rather play with them than wait on their parents." Mary replied. "You're ready to find a good guy and start a family. If Mr. Brad Marshall isn't ready, then it's his loss."

Mary smirked. "You sound like my mother. Did anyone tell you that?"

The sales clerk chuckled, "Once a mother, always a mother."

"Speaking of, Sarah is here."

Morgan walked around the counter, unlocked and opened the door for the young blonde woman to shuffle in. Sarah was slightly out of breath as she entered the door. "Goodness, I swear the walk from the car to the door gets a few feet further every day."

Mary chuckled as Morgan retorted, "I wonder why." Sarah flashed a good-natured smile at the pair.

"Honestly, if you need to sit down and rest, do it." Morgan added.

"Oh, I do." Sarah replied. "Mary keeps a close watch on me."

Mary walked up to the young woman and placed her hand on her arm. "Sarah, Morgan is going to host a baby shower for you."

Sarah glanced at Morgan and her eyes watered. "You don't have to do this."

"You deserve one. Mary has been working on a list and we're talking about having it about a month from now. We need you to go over the list to make sure we haven't overlooked anyone and give us their addresses."

Sarah nodded, wiped her eyes, and then laughed. "I cry at the drop of a hat. It must be all the hormones."

Morgan eyes stung, and she blinked, fighting back the tears that threatened. "You deserve it. Mary and I will handle everything. All you will have to do is show up."

Sarah fished through her purse. "Where's my Kleenex?"

"Here," Morgan replied as she skirted around the display cases, reached the back counter, and pulled out a box.

The younger woman pulled a few tissues and dabbed her eyes before stashing them into a pocket of her slacks. "Let me put my lunch in the fridge and I'll give you a hand." Once Sarah had left the front area, Morgan looked over at Mary. The older woman's eyes had a misty film to them. "Here, you take one too," Morgan added as she thrust the box at salesperson.

Mary nodded and pulled a tissue. "You know, your father is proud of you for taking on management of the store and the fundraiser."

Morgan smiled and blinked her eyes, fighting back another round of tears. "Thanks. When you say that, it means a lot."

Mary reached out and gently patted Morgan's arm. "You're a chip off the old block. Don't ever forget that."

Sarah returned and the trio completed setting up the display cases. Morgan glanced up at the antique clock on the wall. "Ladies, we got some time before the store opens. I'm going down to the Starbucks for a refill. What do you want? My treat."

***

Oh my God! She's here! He struggled with the urge to stand up and approach Morgan, but he couldn't. The conversation on the phone hadn't gone as planned. He'd hoped to be charming, fun, and even witty. So what happened? When Morgan answered the phone his mind went blank.

Another surprise: Morgan's reaction. She should've been nice, even interested. Instead, Morgan hadn't been happy to hear from him. In fact, she'd been a bitch.

Frank averted his eyes and pretended to study his computer screen. He sensed her pass him on her way to the counter. His emotions tossed rational thought around his mind like a kite in a windstorm. He couldn't focus. What should he do? Approach her or wait?

As Morgan placed her order with her back to him, he studied her with sporadic covert glances. She wore slacks today. He preferred her in dresses, they showed off her legs. She had spectacular legs. When alone, he dreamed about Morgan in his arms. Her brown hair would be loose and falling over a pillow, and those long legs would be wrapped around him. In his dreams Morgan wanted him.

He glanced back down to his computer bag. Tucked inside were souvenirs, taken from her car after she hung up on him. Morgan probably didn't know how much she hurt him when she snapped at him and hung up. Her kind never did.

Morgan turned from the counter carrying a tray with three cups on it. He glanced up at her and smiled. "Hi."

She glanced at him and returned the smile. "Hi."

His mind went blank. Say something, the voice in his head screamed. Here was his chance, but all the words hung beyond his reach and left him in crippling silence.

Morgan broke eye contact and within seconds left the café. He exhaled and then took a quick labored draw. To him, when she left, she took the oxygen in the room with her.

Who was the real Morgan Kennedy? Was she the bitch on the phone or the woman who smiled at him and said "hi" to a stranger?

He closed his eyes and angled his head so he could massage his forehead. "Damn," he whispered. *I think I really screwed up.* He opened his eyes, took a sip of his lukewarm coffee and scanned the room. *Wait till she finds out about her car.*

CHAPTER 2

Morgan studied her silver Mercedes. Graceful loops of neon yellow paint snaked around the hood and the sides of the car. In some strange way, the bright cheerful color reminded her of a child's art project except for the word "bitch" scrawled on the driver side door. The contents from the glove compartment lay strewn across the front passenger seat and on the floor. In the back seat, her gym bag sat ripped open.

The two police officers who responded to her call donned gloves before they opened the car's doors. Morgan shifted position to get a better view at the inside. *What was the intruder looking for?* She did a quick silent inventory, and her bra and panties were missing. "Oh my God," she murmured before she pressed her fingers to her lips and her stomach churned.

She glanced over to the officer on the other side of the car as he straightened up after inspecting the front seat. Their eyes locked, and his wary expression sent waves of adrenaline washing through her.

He walked toward her with a calm slow stride as if he didn't have a care in the world, but the concern in his eyes reassured her that he took things seriously. He removed a business card from his pocket. "Ms. Kennedy, I'm Officer Romano. Any idea who did this?"

Morgan took a deep breath. *What would he think about her answer?* "Maybe."

The officer cocked an eyebrow. "Can you explain that?"

She raked her hand through her hair. "I came back to the store today from an out-of-town business trip and found several messages on my voice mail. The caller didn't say anything specific. He just called and hung up. I deleted them and chalked it up to someone calling the wrong number. Until later this morning when I answered the phone and we spoke."

"What did he say?"

"Don't leave me again." Morgan crossed her arms and searched the officer's face in hopes of reading his response. "The man was creepy. I hung up on him," she added with a shrug.

"Did you recognize the man's voice?"

"No. But I wrote down the phone number and even tried doing a reverse phone look-up." Morgan paused and waited as the officer finished writing. "I thought if I could find out who he was, I'd report him to you," she added.

"Do you still have the number?"

She nodded and blinked, her eyes fighting the sting which promised tears. "I thought this was a practical joke."

"Doesn't look like it," the officer replied. "This is no random act of vandalism." His eyes swung around and he pointed to the driver's side door. "This is personal. Is anything missing?

Morgan gulped. "I can't be sure about the glove compartment. I keep receipts for car repairs in there. But I think he took some articles of clothing."

"What did he take?"

Personal. The term pinged through her mind. Morgan gulped and took a shaky breath. "He took my bra and panties." She closed her eyes, raised her hand, and rubbed her forehead.

"Have you had an argument with anyone you know lately? What about a disgruntled customer or boyfriend?"

Morgan glanced away from the officer's gaze and stared at the cumulus clouds above the mountains in the distance. She knew where this line of questions would lead, and no matter what she said, the police would think he did this.

Officer Romano didn't push her for a response. He waited. His restraint and the yawning silence applied even more pressure on her.

"I did break up with my boyfriend recently. But I'm certain he didn't do this. This type of thing isn't his style."

She cringed at her last remark. *Not his style?* Her comment sounded like she belonged on some pseudo reality TV show. "Officer, what I meant to say is he has no reason to do this."

Doubt flickered through the officer's eyes. "Would you mind if we contact him?"

Morgan dropped her crossed arms to her sides. Over the past few minutes, the shock of what happened had faded. Her temples throbbed as she wiped the beads of sweat from her brow. Now frustration and anger had arrived fueling what promised to be a major headache.

"Excuse me, Officer. Can we step inside the store?"

The policeman flashed a polite smile and nodded to the store's back entrance, "After you."

Morgan opened the door to the jewelry store and a blast of cool air rolled out. Once inside, she turned and faced the officer.

"Look, the break up with my boyfriend was mutual, and we haven't had any problems at the store."

"What's the name of your boyfriend?"

"Ex-boyfriend," Morgan corrected.

She glared at the officer and then realized he evaluated not only her answers but her physical response. *He doesn't believe me*, she thought as she tamped down the urge to scream, *hey I'm the victim here.*

She sighed. "His name is Brad Marshall. He's a partner at Marshall, Lyons and Smith in downtown Phoenix."

The officer hesitated before writing the name down on his pad, and she quickly moved her hand up to her lips to hide her smirk. The policeman recognized the firm's name. They specialized in criminal defense and last year they were at the center of a media firestorm as they represented a man charged as a serial killer. As a partner in the firm, there was no way her former boyfriend would drive to Scottsdale on a Tuesday morning to vandalize her car.

The officer fidgeted with the pen. "When was the last time the two of you communicated?"

Morgan crossed her arms. "I don't know, maybe two or three weeks ago."

The officer scribbled on his notepad again. "What about your mystery caller? Could you have met him at an event or a club?"

"No," Morgan replied. "I don't do the club scene anymore."

She crossed her arms and waited for the next question. The officer's assumption was a popular one. As part of a family that owned a successful jewelry store and who actively worked on charity projects, people thought she led a life of leisure, juggling manicures and lunches. The truth was far less glamorous. She studied at the Gemological Institute of America and when her father had a heart attack several months back she shelved her jewelry design work to take on day-to-day store management.

The officer slowly closed the notepad. "Can you give us the phone number you wrote down? We'll investigate and get back in touch with you."

"Of course," Morgan strode into her office, retrieved the crumbled sheet of paper from her trash can and unfurled it. She handed it to the officer, "Here."

The officer looked briefly at the number before placing it in the notepad. "We'll check for a match on the fingerprints left on your car. But don't get your hopes up. In the meantime, you need to be more careful and above all, make sure you lock your car."

Morgan nodded and hoped the policeman didn't see her cringe. *Idiot! You forgot to lock your car.*

She forced a smile. "Thank you Officer Romano, I'll be more careful."

Morgan trailed behind him as he exited out of the store's back door. The other policeman had finished dusting for fingerprints and had packed up. Within minutes, they'd left.

Morgan stood in the doorway and surveyed her vehicle. She was stranded. Imagine the stares she'd get with the word "bitch" plastered on the driver's side. "That would be great publicity for the fundraiser."

She turned around and let the back door close and lock behind her as she headed to her office. With the dinner and auction in three days, the first order of business was a rental car, and a tow truck to take her vehicle to the dealership. After making those arrangements, Morgan left her office and went out to the front of the store. She nodded at Mary who stood behind the counter. "How's it been?"

"Busy. We've had quite a bit of pre-charity auction window shopping."

Morgan grinned. "I'm glad to hear that."

Mary crooked a knowing smile. "You shouldn't worry. The auction will be a big success."

"Tell my father," Morgan quipped. "He's convinced that no one can do it as well as he can."

Sarah padded in from the back rooms and rubbed her back. "Who are you talking about?"

Morgan smiled. "My father."

"He's a force of nature," Sarah replied. "Can I ask you a question?"

"Sure," Morgan said.

"Why did your family start the Diamonds in the Desert Fundraiser?"

Mary coughed, and Sarah shot a quick glance over at the older woman. Mary pressed her lips together and shook her head. "Oh, I'm sorry. I didn't realize." Sarah stammered.

"No," Morgan replied. "It's okay." She flashed a quick smile at Mary. "My parents started the Diamonds in the Desert Fundraiser a couple years after my brother's death. They wanted to ensure no family had to bear what we did after my brother, Samuel's, swimming accident."

Sarah's expression became somber. "What happened?"

Morgan paused. She'd not been asked about what happened for many years and yet, the pain still felt fresh.

Sarah put her hands up. "It's okay if you don't want to talk about it."

Morgan reached out to touch the pregnant woman. "No. I want to."

She took a couple seconds to collect her thoughts. "My brother had always been adventurous, sometimes even reckless. Samuel and I were swimming in the pool and he'd been clowning around. He tried a back flip off the diving board and struck his head."

"Oh my God," Sarah said. She looked at Mary and then back at Morgan. "I didn't know you were there."

Sarah's eyes watered, and Morgan pressed her fingers to her lips and then dropped them. "I jumped in and dragged him over to the side of the pool. I kept his head above water so he could breathe. I screamed for help. My mother heard me and pulled him out of the pool. He never regained consciousness." Morgan gulped and glanced away from Sarah. The young woman was a breath away from tears, and if Sarah lost it, Morgan would too.

"But God made lemonade out of lemons." Mary said.

Morgan and Sarah stared at the mature saleswoman. "What?" Sarah asked.

"Samuel's death was a tragedy but you honor his life with this fundraiser. Your family has raised millions of dollars over the years. Think of the lives you have saved with the equipment your auction has paid for."

"Yes," Sarah added.

Morgan smiled and swallowed, but the lump in her throat stubbornly refused to relax. "Uh, I've got a tow truck coming for my car and I need to arrange a ride to pick up a rental."

Mary asked, "Do the police have any clues as to who did this?"

"Nothing solid," Morgan replied.

"I'll tell you, the world is going to Hell in a hand basket. Why would someone do something like that?" The older woman asked.

"I don't know," Morgan replied. "I'm going to give Stella a call and see if she can give me a ride. If you need me, I'll be in my office."

***

"Hey Stella, I need a favor."

"Depends, what's up?"

Morgan smiled at the joking response on the other end of the line. Despite the teasing, her best friend would grant her request.

"Can you give me a ride to go pick up a rental car?"

"Sure, for a price. Chinese?"

Morgan laughed. "You're on! Can you be here around four?"

"Sure, but why do you need a rental car?"

"We've had a little problem with vandalism. I'll give you the details when you get here."

"Strange, I didn't peg your neighborhood as having this type of problem."

"Me neither," Morgan said.

A few minutes past four, Stella pulled up in front of the store and Morgan, who had been watching for Stella's SUV through the storefront window, quickly stepped outside to slide into the passenger side of the vehicle.

"Okay, what happened?"

Morgan glanced at her friend. Concern graced her eyes and tinged her voice.

"Someone spray painted my car and stole some clothing out of my gym bag."

"Oh my God, when did this happen?"

"Between when I came in to set up the store this morning and left for lunch around noon. I thought I'd locked the car, but apparently I didn't. The intruder went through the car, even my gym bag and took my bra and panties."

"Did you file a police report?"

"Yep, but they weren't too encouraging. The bottom line is I shouldn't expect much. They even thought Brad did this."

"Morgan, you can't blame them for asking. I'm sure they deal with this all the time. Disgruntled former boyfriends or husbands probably account for the majority of people who do these types of things."

"I know, but the decision to break up was mutual. We want different things," Morgan replied quietly as she glanced out the side window avoiding her friend's appraising gaze. She wasn't ready to talk about the break-up with anyone at this point, not even Stella.

After twenty minutes in traffic, Stella pulled up to the car rental office, and Morgan slid out of the front seat. "Almond chicken?"

"Absolutely."

"All right, give me an hour and meet me at my place. I've got to tape the TV interview tomorrow for the fundraiser, and I must make a final decision on what to wear. I need your advice."

"You're asking me? I live in jeans all day," Stella said.

"But they're such *nice* jeans."

Morgan admired her friend's style. Despite working for her family's construction company, Stella was always pulled together and fashionable.

"Don't forget the egg rolls," Stella added as she started to close the door.

"Morgan?"

She leaned in to glance at Stella and noted the humor had faded from her eyes. "Yes?"

"Be careful."

CHAPTER 3

"Stella, you shouldn't have done this," Morgan smiled as she took the vase with the pink roses and baby's breath from her friend's hands.

"Wish I could take credit, but they were on the doorstep when I arrived," Stella replied. "Do you think that Brad sent them?"

Morgan grinned as she carried the flowers to the kitchen and set them on the counter. She leaned in, inhaled their delicate fragrance and removed the small pastel envelope from the bouquet. She cast a quick glance and smiled at her friend. "Who else would send me my favorite flowers?"

"Go ahead, open it." Stella said.

Morgan's smile faded as she glanced at her friends face. Stella didn't appear happy. In fact, she seemed outright concerned.

"You'll see." Morgan peeled the flap back on the small envelope, slid the card out and read the message. "What the…"

She blinked and reread the message. The note was written in blue ink and printed in childlike script. "Sorry about the car. I'll see you around."

"Well," Stella said.

Morgan glanced up at her friend and drew a quick, deep breath, "Dear God, he's been here." She peered over her shoulder first left, then right. *Was he inside the house?* If this were a horror movie, here was the part where her stalker would jump out of a closet with a knife or gun.

Stella snatched the card, "Morgan, give me that."

Morgan's mind replayed the scenario of her coming home and finding him waiting for her. She stared blankly at the flowers.

"This came from the guy who tagged your car?" Stella asked.

Morgan nodded, "yeah."

"Give me the details of what happened today. Start from the beginning."

Morgan took another deep breath and recounted to Stella the activities of the day. Stella's blue eyes usually sparkled with humor and merriment, but the concern there ignited an edgy buzz in Morgan. Her first instinct was to dash to the rental car and run. But the fear of what might await her in the shadows kept her in the house.

"You must call the police," Stella said.

Morgan snapped her gaze away from the flowers. "Huh?"

"Police. Call them," Stella ordered.

Morgan nodded and removed Officer Romano's card out of her wallet and quickly dialed the number. She left a quick message, and after ending the call, she looked at her friend. "Stella, what am I going to do? I'm not sure they can be much help because I have no idea who this man is."

Stella fingered the note as she considered the question. After a few moments, she fished her cell phone out of her purse, "Let me call someone who owns a security company. His firm worked on the vandalism and theft problems we had last year, but they also handle personal protection for many bands and their concerts. Maybe he can help us."

***

Shawn jerked. The phone's ring broke the silence of the empty office and his concentration. "Not now," he murmured as he tried to focus on the laptop in front of him. The schedule for the security staff for the concert should have been posted yesterday, and the last thing he needed was another interruption. He'd deal with the message tomorrow. As the recorded introduction to his voice mailbox played, the phone disconnected, and within seconds his cell phone rang.

He glanced at the caller ID. *Adams Construction.* "Damn," Shawn growled as he punched the button. "Sonoran Security."

"Shawn?" The woman sounded nervous.

"Speaking."

"Shawn, this is Stella Adams. I'm sorry to intrude at this hour, but I need your expertise on a situation. Can we meet tonight?"

Shawn softly massaged his forehead as he stared at the computer screen in front of him. She probably had another construction site issue. He'd let her lay it out over the phone and schedule a meeting for tomorrow. "What's the problem?"

"My friend is being stalked."

Whoa. He glanced up from the laptop and leaned back in his chair for a few seconds. *So much for construction site security.* Shawn took a deep breath of air, "Did your friend contact the police and file a restraining order?"

"Police report, yes. Restraining order, well that's a problem. She doesn't know who the stalker is." Stella replied.

He shot a quick look at his wristwatch and calculated how quickly he could finish. "Okay, give me a couple hours. What's the address?"

Stella paused and spoke to someone off line. A feminine voice replied, and Stella repeated the directions as he scribbled them on a notepad.

"Thanks, I really appreciate you coming out tonight." Stella said.

The young woman's voice literally dripped with concern. "What's your friend's name?"

Stella replied, "Kennedy. Morgan Kennedy."

Shawn closed his eyes and rubbed his brow. The publicity for the upcoming fundraiser for the children's hospital had been splashed in the newspapers and he had a vague recollection of reading an article about the daughter chairing the event. "Okay, I'll be there as soon as I can." He added, "In the meantime, make sure the doors are locked and stay put."

"Got it," Stella replied and then she ended the call.

Stalked? The word pinged through his mind and memories from Southern California flooded his thoughts like the aftermath of a dam break. He hadn't dealt with a stalking case in years.

***

Morgan listened as Stella talked to Shawn and the gravity of the situation began to sink in. *Stalker.* The word conjured up visions of the Michael Myers character from the *Halloween* movies. Morgan reined in her imagination and forced herself to glance at her friend. "Thanks. I had no idea what was happening until today."

"Why would you," Stella asked as she opened a bottle of pinot grigio and poured the wine. "Here, I think you could use this." Her friend handed her a glass. "Now you need to have some food."

Morgan took several sips, "I'm not hungry." Her glance darted over to the vase. *How did he know pink roses were her favorite?* Normally she would be delighted with such a gift, but this wasn't a gift, the flowers were an apology. "Sorry about the car." Did this idiot have any idea what repainting her Mercedes would cost? Resentment bubbled up, and she defiantly picked up the vase, went outside of the house to the garbage can and dropped them inside. *Apology not accepted.*

When she returned, Stella had removed the takeout boxes from the sacks and handed a plate to her. "Eat," her friend ordered.

Morgan hesitated. She wasn't hungry, but the beginning of an alcohol buzz crept over her. She needed to put something other than wine in her stomach or she'd be completely tipsy by the time Stella's security specialist arrived. Morgan set the glass down, picked up a spoon, and scooped rice onto her plate.

"Here," Stella said as she handed Morgan the warm carton. Morgan opened the box and the aroma of chicken and sauce wafted out. Her stomach rolled like an ice cream maker. She glanced up. Her friend was removing the egg rolls from the paper wrapper and placed one on her plate. "I'm not sure I can."

"Start with the rice, work your way through the vegetables, and then the chicken. If your stomach doesn't settle, skip the egg roll. I'll make some tea."

Morgan picked up the fork and began to work on the rice. Within a few minutes, her stomach had calmed down and she picked at the entree.

"So, what are you planning to wear tomorrow?"

Morgan watched as her friend set a kettle on the stove and pulled out a teapot and teabags from the pantry. "I've narrowed it to a few choices. But I want to be sure that I don't pick something too cocktail-like."

The tall blonde poured the hot water into the teapot and cast a quick glance at her before sprouting a small grin. "The woman who probably invented the buttoned-up businesswoman look? This shouldn't be too hard."

"Thanks. I knew I could count on you for moral support." Morgan took another forkful of chicken and vegetables. Despite her friend's efforts to keep things light and off the topic of her stalker, she battled the urge to glance out of the window.

"Morgan, relax." Stella handed her a cup of steaming tea. "Shawn will be here in a couple of hours. I'm not going anywhere. Tonight we'll get some counsel and a game plan pulled together. Right now, let's enjoy our meal."

Morgan smiled at her friend. "Yes, Mother."

After dinner, the pair spent the next hour reviewing Morgan's wardrobe options for the interview. They narrowed five dresses down to two and Morgan eventually decided on a royal blue wrap dress. She was picking the dresses up off of her bed to return them to the closet when the doorbell rang.

Morgan jumped and glanced at Stella. Her friend smiled. "Relax. It's going to be okay."

Morgan nodded. "Could you please let him in?"

After Stella left the room, Morgan put away the remaining pieces of clothing. A shiver rippled through her, and she slowly glanced over to the window. The drapes to the bedroom were drawn, and no one could see in, yet she sensed he was out there in the dark, watching.

"Quit," she whispered to herself as she straightened her blouse and finger combed her hair. "I'll get through this."

She walked to the living room and waited. She heard Stella open the door and say, "Shawn, thanks for coming." Her friend's voice dropped, and Morgan could not make out the low masculine reply. She cocked her head to the right in hopes of catching more of the conversation. The discussion paused and within moments Stella entered the room with a man following her.

Morgan studied the man and an electric crackle sizzled through her. The only experience she had with security personnel were the middle-aged, paunchy guards who came to the store to pick up money and jewelry for transport. This man was a whole different breed of animal. He moved with a quiet grace as he scanned the surroundings, taking them in, before focusing on her. His dark brown hair was cut short, and the dusting of gray at his temples lent an air of experience about him.

His eyes were crystal blue and had an edge to them which left her with the impression that they missed little and had seen much. For a brief moment, a flicker of appreciation appeared as he studied her. Almost instantly, the expression faded, and cool analytical detachment replaced it. Morgan's mouth went dry. She didn't know anything about him, but from the "don't mess with me" aura he exuded, she'd bet he was former military, police, or both.

He extended his hand. "I'm Shawn Randall from Sonoran Security. How can I be of assistance?"

Morgan stepped forward and shook it. "Morgan Kennedy. I'm glad to meet you."

A small smirk broke on his lips and the irony of what she had said hit her. He took her hand. Attraction and nervousness sent an adrenaline surge coursing through her. She searched his eyes, hoping for an indication he had the same reaction, but he regarded her with calm scrutiny.

I'm being studied like some insect. She pulled back and crossed her arms defensively. Taking a shaky breath, she wondered what she should say next. *Just give him the facts.*

She willed herself to stay calm as she explained, "I've got a stalker. I don't know who he is, but this morning he vandalized my car. This afternoon, he sent flowers to my home as an apology. The police haven't been terribly encouraging. I don't know what to do."

There. She said it. A short, simple, direct reply. Morgan blinked as she fought to hold back the tears.

"Okay, let's start from the beginning." His voice possessed a patient polite tone which echoed the policeman's conversation earlier today.

Morgan gestured for Shawn to sit in a nearby chair, and she sat opposite him on the sofa. She took a deep breath and began to recount the activities in detail. Shawn listened. Only when she detailed her car's vandalism did he stop her.

"What did he take?"

Morgan stopped and tucked a strand of her hair behind her ear. "He stole some clothes out of my gym bag."

"What kind of clothing?"

She pondered how to phrase her answer. *Exactly how do you tell someone you met less than five minutes ago a stalker took your bra and panties?*

"Did he take lingerie?" Shawn asked.

Morgan gulped and heat flushed her face. "Yes. He took my bra and panties."

Shawn nodded and sat back from the edge of his chair. "So, he has a souvenir."

Morgan snorted a laugh, "That's an odd way to phrase it."

Shawn grinned. "Yeah, I know. But you have to remember today he talked to you. He made personal contact, and although taking your clothes is the type of thing which will freak you out, it's a trophy to him. What did the police say?"

"Not much, because I can't identify this guy. Unless they get a fingerprint match, I'm out of luck. Do you have any suggestions? At this point, I don't feel safe."

"Good," Shawn replied.

"Excuse me?" Morgan couldn't keep the incredulous tone out of her voice.

"Trust your instincts on this. You're not safe."

Morgan glanced over at Stella, whose expression mirrored Morgan's shock. She turned back at Shawn. "This is crazy. How can I make him go away?"

"When he's caught, or when he moves on to a new victim."

Victim. The word pinged through her mind and made her feel uneasy. She managed a retail store, staff, and one of the largest fundraisers in the metropolitan area. She helped victims, Morgan never thought she'd be one.

Shawn leaned forward, and Morgan detected sympathy in his demeanor and voice. "I don't want to add fuel to the fire but here's how it goes. You didn't know until today, but you've had a stalker for some time. He's followed you, knows your routine, what you do, and where you live. I've worked in the personal security business for a number of years. It happens to celebrities often. Most of their fans are harmless, but occasionally, they get stalkers too."

"Well, I'm no movie star. Why me?"

"If I had the answer to that question, I'd be rich. We aren't dealing with a normal person here. Thanks to the fundraiser's publicity, he's fixated on you. In fact, not being a celebrity has worked to your disadvantage. He's had an easy time tracking you."

Morgan glanced over at Stella and caught her friend's alarmed expression. "How do I stop him?"

"You start taking precautions. I have a few ground rules you'll need to follow. Then be prepared, it'll get worse, maybe a lot worse. But if we're ready, we'll catch him and get him out of your life."

Stella spoke up for the first time, "What does she need to do?"

Shawn cast a quick glance to Stella and returned to Morgan. "Are you hiring me?"

Morgan glanced at Stella.

"You should. This is getting out of control," Stella urged.

She looked at Shawn. He waited for her response, and a little flicker of irritation rippled through her. She glanced down and fingered the green tourmaline ring on her right finger. "Too fast," the voice in her head warned. Her first instinct was to resist. Think things through, have a plan. She didn't have to do this. "No thank you" was an option. But since the phone calls this morning, she'd been dancing to her stalker's tune. When he made his next move, then what? She pressed her lips together and took a deep breath. "Yes, I suppose I am."

Shawn nodded. "Okay. I'll have a contract sent over to the store for your review and approval. We'll need your signature tomorrow."

Morgan stared at her new bodyguard and tamped down her immediate reflex to stand up and say she'd changed her mind. His no-nonsense attitude reassured and irritated her at the same time.

"What does Morgan need to do?" Stella asked again.

Shawn leaned forward in his chair. "Okay, first, no contact. Let your phone calls go to voicemail so they can be screened. We don't want to encourage him by letting him talk to you. Next, vary your routine. Mix things up and he'll be thrown off balance. Then we gain the advantage. Last, you'll amp up the security. I'm assuming the jewelry store has an excellent system, but what about here?"

"I have an alarm and a monitoring service." Morgan replied.

"Deadbolts on the doors?"

"Yes."

Shawn rose from his chair. "Good. Let's take a quick walk through. I want to make sure everything is locked and all's clear."

Morgan stood up. "Where do you want to start?"

"Let's start with the garage and the entrance," Shawn said.

Morgan paused. Should she lead the way or would he? She waited for him to make the first move for a few seconds, then she cracked a nervous smile. "Follow me."

For the next twenty minutes, the trio went from room to room as Shawn checked locks and possible hiding places. Once the inspection was completed, they returned to the living room.

"I want Matt, my partner, to come and check the outside and evaluate how we can make things more secure. Tonight, one of our security cars will patrol your house several times. What are your plans for tomorrow?"

"I have to tape a television interview at KDEZ at eleven a.m."

"Okay, I'll pick you up at nine. From now on, when you are out in public, someone from Sonoran Security will be with you."

"Morgan, do you want me to stay with you tonight?" Stella asked.

Morgan smiled at her friend, thankful for her moral support. "No, I'll be okay."

Stella looked over at Shawn.

"You and Morgan can decide. With the house locked up and the security car outside Morgan won't be in any danger," he said.

"Stella, you don't have to stay."

Stella paused. "Are you sure? I have to be at a home inspection in Chandler at eight a.m., but I can reschedule."

"No, don't cancel. Go home and get a good night's sleep."

"All right, but if something happens or you change your mind, call me."

"Right after him," Morgan replied nodding in Shawn's direction.

Stella picked up her purse and stood up to leave. "Shawn thanks for coming over. Tell Matt I said, hi."

Shawn flashed a relaxed smile at Stella, "Will do."

Morgan noted his blue eyes twinkled as he smiled. She wondered if there was some unspoken conversation going on between the two of them. They'd worked together for a while last year and shortly after, Stella broke up with her boyfriend.

"I need to be leaving too." Shawn said.

They headed for the front door with Morgan bringing up the rear. Opening the door, Stella leaned forward and gave Morgan a sisterly hug. "Take care, I'll call tomorrow." She turned and walked out to her vehicle.

Morgan glanced at Shawn as he stepped up to her. "When I leave, set the alarm. Here's my card. If anything happens, call the police and then me. The police can get to you faster than I can. Do you have any questions?"

"Shawn, you said things will get worse. What am I in for?"

The relaxed look that he had when he spoke with Stella faded and the no-nonsense attitude re-appeared. "I don't know," he answered quietly.

Morgan crossed her arms as a chill settled on her shoulders and back. She took a slow breath, "You're not reassuring."

Shawn nodded and the corners of his lips curled up. "I'm sorry, but these types of things are unpredictable. Good night."

She closed and locked the door behind him. Curious, she peered out through the security peephole and observed Shawn as he talked to Stella for a few brief moments. After Stella walked to her SUV, Shawn pulled out his cell, and dialed a number as he headed toward his vehicle.

She heard the engine start and a dark Escalade passed the front entrance before disappearing from her line of sight. She turned and walked back to the living room and stopped at the arcadia door. The lights of Cave Creek twinkled in the distance, and she knew he was out there. She sensed him.

***

Hidden in the shadows every night, he watched, waited and worshipped. Who needed cable TV? All they offered was a conga line of interchangeable bleached blondes. Those shows portrayed them as smart, beautiful, and rich, but he knew better. Morgan was the real thing and perfect for him. They belonged together.

Tonight she'd left the drapes pulled back. He saw her dump the flowers and eat take out with her friend. Who was the new guy? He wasn't family or Morgan's ex-boyfriend Brad. That jerk had been out of the picture for several weeks now. Was this another boyfriend? Resentment and possessiveness coursed through his veins with each heartbeat. *Mine.*

"Come on. I need to see you, just one more time." He whispered and as if God heard his plea, Morgan appeared at the arcadia door and stared into the darkness. "Soon baby, soon," he murmured. She reached over and began to draw the blinds.

"No, No," he whined. "A little longer, please." Morgan never heard him and closed them. "Show's over" the voice in his head announced. He sighed and moved back from behind the dense shrub surrounding the ironwood tree. The undergrowth provided excellent cover. The access was even better. All he had to do was go a few hundred feet down the dry wash to his car.

He trekked slowly down the sandy trail in darkness. He couldn't use a flashlight and risk discovery. Off to his left, the brush rustled. Startled, he paused and listened closely. Whatever the animal was, it moved away from him, and he exhaled in relief. The desert came alive after dark as the predators hunted in the coolness and cover of the night. He wouldn't have to hide out in the shadows much longer. *We'll be together in just three days.*

CHAPTER 4

"Matt, this is Shawn. We've got a new client, give me a call."

Shawn set the phone down on the console between the driver and passenger seat. His partner would have to pick up the concert job, in addition to the inspection. The lion's share of his time and attention for the foreseeable future had just been commissioned. If this had been a standard security assignment, he'd be very comfortable turning this case over to the team, but Stella Adams' call was a personal request. She was one of a handful of people in the valley who knew his professional background would make him the perfect candidate to protect her friend.

How would Matt take it when he found out Stella had entered the picture again? Last year, his partner worked with her family to resolve some construction site theft problems. His interest in the blue-eyed blonde had been obvious, but she'd been dating someone else at the time, and Matt stepped back from any personal entanglement. His business partner had been smart and stuck to business. Shawn pressed his lips together and tightened his grip on the steering wheel. On the other hand, it seemed he always needed to learn his lessons the hard way.

He thought about the current case. Nothing is tougher than dealing with an unidentified stalker. At least if the client knows who is stalking them, you know who you need to be on guard against. They have a name, face, address, history, and patterns of behavior. With this case, he'd be on the defensive until they figured out the stalker's identity.

His most recent experience occurred a couple years back when he'd guarded a well-known recording artist who came to party at the Super Bowl events. Before the celebrity arrived in town, Shawn had received a folder on "questionable" fans. The folder contained a long list of people, but what concerned Shawn most was the "wild card", the unpredictable and possibly dangerous person whose name wasn't on the list.

Shawn took a deep breath as he remembered what happened. A young woman showed up and demanded to be let into the VIP area. She claimed to be an invited close friend and threatened to get anyone who stood in her way fired. The security team did what they'd been trained to do and denied her access, but the woman refused to be stopped. As the stand-off worsened, Shawn made the call and had her removed from the club. His last vision of the fan was still crystal clear. She'd stood in the parking lot with tears running down her face. Once outside, she pounded on the door and screamed to be let back inside. She disappeared only after the police showed up.

When Shawn first walked into Morgan's house, he braced himself for another socialite who probably had hooked up with some "admirer wannabe boyfriend" at a local club. He'd figured that when the relationship ended, things went bad.

Morgan Kennedy surprised him. She met him wearing jeans and a cotton top. As the owner-manager of one of the most prestigious jewelry stores in the valley, she could have easily overdone the bling, but she hadn't. She sported a nice dress watch, a ring and a pair of diamond stud earrings.

She even seemed embarrassed to admit the stalker had taken lingerie. Her uncomfortable response to this question left no doubt in his mind she did nothing to create her current situation.

The cell phone rang, and he picked it up, "Yeah."

"Fill me in." Matt said.

Shawn brought his partner up to speed on the case.

"I'll call Bill. He's on patrol in north Scottsdale tonight, and he can swing by her house a few times over the next eight hours," Matt said.

"Thanks. I will be escorting Ms. Kennedy to her interview at KDEZ tomorrow, so you'll have to take the lead on the concert preparations. Oh, before I forget, I ran into a Stella Adams tonight. She said hi."

A long pause followed before Matt spoke. "How is she?"

"She's fine."

"How is Stella involved in this case?"

"She's a good friend of Ms. Kennedy."

Matt exhaled. "Okay. I'll be there at ten a.m. for a security review."

"Thanks." Shawn ended the call and set the phone on the passenger seat. He knew his partner well and even though Matt didn't say anything specific, he didn't need to. Morgan's stalker posed a threat to anyone around her. One person to protect is a challenge, safeguarding two or more made an assignment exponentially harder. This case had the potential of getting ugly. Shawn could feel it in his gut.

***

Morgan sat perched on a stool at the breakfast counter in the kitchen and clicked the remote as reruns and infomercials popped up one after another. "Unbelievable. Over one hundred channels and there's nothing to watch," Morgan muttered as she turned off the TV. She picked up the coffee mug and sipped the brew in a desperate hope that more caffeine would chase away the heavy exhaustion which hung on her.

After Stella and Shawn had left, Morgan showered and went to bed only to toss, turn, and lie awake for most of the night. She had turned down Stella's offer to stay with her. After all, she was a grown woman and the bodyguard had said she'd be safe, but every creak the house made sent her heart racing. When a dust storm rolled through and the windows rattled with the wind gusts, she'd laid in bed and listened. Around two a.m. Morgan finally gave up and turned on the cable news stations before she relaxed enough to slip into a light sleep.

Her eyes traveled over to the clock on the digital receiver. Eight forty-five. Shawn should be here shortly. If someone had told her yesterday morning she'd be sitting at home twenty-four hours later waiting for her bodyguard, Morgan would've thought they were nuts. She placed the cup in the dishwasher and went to the master bedroom.

She walked into the adjoining bathroom, flipped on the light and studied her reflection. The deep royal blue wrap dress Stella insisted she wear highlighted her fair complexion and dark brown hair.

The door bell sounded. "Showtime," Morgan whispered as she turned off the lights, picked up her purse and walked to the door. Butterflies danced in her stomach, and she instinctively placed her hand on her belly. Why was she nervous? Could it be the interview, the stalker or him? *No, not him.* She paused and closed her eyes. "Focus, you have a job to do." She barely reached the front entry when the doorbell chimed a second time. She peered through the security peephole.

The mid-morning sun shone and Shawn stood several feet back from the front door studying the nearby desert. He wore a gray suit with a white shirt and he appeared taller than she remembered from last night. Morgan opened the door. Shawn turned and gave her a quick once over. A nervous tremor rippled in the wake of his gaze and Morgan uttered a silent prayer that the outfit she had chosen for the interview would meet his approval. Stella told her Shawn had done some security work for people in the entertainment industry. If her dress was wrong, he'd probably peg her as an amateur, and for some reason she didn't quite fathom at this moment, that thought irritated her.

A smile softened the firm line of his lips. "Ready?"

Morgan relaxed. "Yes, let me set the alarm." She quickly closed the front door, punched in the code and then stepped out, locking it behind her. "Let's go."

Morgan turned and walked toward his SUV with Shawn at her side. He moved with a quiet grace which caused the butterflies to dance again. She cast a quick glance at him and caught him surveying the street beyond her front yard. *Say something*, the little voice in her head prodded. "Quite a dust storm last night."

She cringed. *Geez Morgan, you're being stalked and the first topic of conversation with your new bodyguard is the weather?* She gulped and continued to march toward the passenger side of the vehicle.

"Yeah, it was a bad one. The patrol cars reported that besides the storm, everything was quiet."

Morgan chuckled. "Yes. But thanks to my vivid imagination, every time the wind rattled the windows I thought of my stalker."

She reached his SUV, stopped and craned her neck up to peer at him. He crooked a slightly guilty smile. "I wondered about that. You appeared so confident when you told Stella she didn't have to stay last night. You've got quite a poker face." Shawn reached over and opened the door.

"Thanks," Morgan said as she slid in. She buckled her seat belt and fought the urge to study him walk around to the driver's side. *This may not be as bad as I imagined.*

Shawn sat down on the driver's side, reached down and handed her a manila envelope. "Here is the contract for the security services."

"Oh, uh, okay." Morgan replied as she took the envelope, peeled the flap back and slid the document out. She stared at the page trying to focus on the words in front of her as Shawn started the ignition and pulled out of the driveway. Within minutes, they were traveling west toward Cave Creek Road.

"Okay, fill me in. What's the schedule today?"

Morgan glanced up from the papers. "The interview is at eleven. Then, I need to go to Copper Creek Resort to review the furniture set up for the party. Then, back at the store by four to meet with our web designer. We're launching the online part of the auction tonight."

"I thought the fundraiser was a dinner and an auction."

"You're correct, for a few of the big ticket items. However, to raise the kind of money we're striving for, we need to reach a larger audience so we'll have approximately two hundred items from electronics to dinners at local restaurants available for bid on an Internet auction."

"Doesn't the jewelry auction bring most of the money?"

Morgan smiled at him. "You may not believe this, but I'm projecting over sixty percent of the funds we'll raise will come from more modest-priced items."

"Impressive, your idea?"

Morgan slid the contract back in the envelope. "Yes, I lobbied for it years ago, but dad wasn't sure we should do it. When I took over the event, I decided to move ahead on this part of the fundraiser."

"Is your father still active in the jewelry store?"

"Not anymore. He had a heart attack a few months ago and had to slow down. He keeps saying he will never retire, but the truth is we only see him at the store about once every couple weeks. He plays golf nearly every day though."

Shawn grinned. "Kinda sounds like he's substituted golf for work."

Morgan smiled. "You have a point. Mom says as long as he limits it to eighteen holes a day she'll deal with it."

"Do you have any brothers or sisters?"

"My younger sister, Vicki, is a grad student at ASU, studying archeology."

"An archeologist? I would've thought she'd go into the family business too."

"So did Dad. Her decision shocked him, but he got over it. How about you? Got any siblings?"

"One younger brother, he's in the Marines and is overseas right now."

"Have you heard from him recently?"

"About six weeks ago," Shawn replied quietly.

Morgan fingered the papers in her hand and studied Shawn. He straightened up in his seat and his right index finger tapped on the steering wheel.

"You must be very proud of him," she added. She pressed her lips together after she spoke. Her comment sounded like such a cliché response.

"We are, but he needs to come home. This is his second tour. He's done enough."

"We?"

"Yeah, my parents supported him when he made the decision to join, but they won't rest easy till he's back home."

Shawn glanced up in the rear view mirror and frowned. Morgan bit her lip and looked out the side window. In an effort to be friendly, she broached a sensitive subject. Now Shawn had shut down. Morgan glanced down and pulled out the contract. *Note to self: Don't get too personal with the hired help.*

***

The older model burgundy Japanese import had trailed behind them since shortly after they left Morgan's house. Custom and semi-custom homes on acre-plus lots dotted the desert. This car didn't fit in. Shawn considered whether to ask Morgan if she had seen this car around before.

Who are you? He gently pushed down on the accelerator and put some distance between them and the vehicle. The car dropped back and then sped up to close the gap. His heart pounded and adrenaline coursed through him. Was it going to be this simple? Could this be her stalker? He glanced over at Morgan. She was focused on studying the contract.

Okay, let's get a look at you, he thought. He lifted his foot off the accelerator and glanced back. As if the driver realized he was too close, the car dropped back.

A soft metallic blue BMW pulled out from another side road and settled between Shawn's SUV and the Honda. As they reached the stoplight, he double-checked the rearview mirror. The BMW driver was a woman on a cell phone, and he couldn't get a clear look at the car behind her. The light changed, and he turned south on Cave Creek Road.

Impatient to get a better view, Shawn pulled over to the outside lane, slowed down before pulling onto the gravel, and stopped. He stared in the rear view mirror as the lady in the BMW passed him and the economy car cleared the intersection.

He glanced over to Morgan, who gazed back with a puzzled expression.

"Don't turn around," he said quietly.

Her face paled, "Oh my God. Is it him?"

"Not sure," Shawn said as he looked back in the mirror.

The Honda slowed down and pulled into a Circle K convenience store and stopped at a gas pump.

"False alarm," Morgan said with an air of relief in her voice. Shawn glanced over and noticed she'd pulled down the sun visor and used the vanity mirror to watch.

"Maybe," Shawn replied as he gave the import car one last check before pulling back on the asphalt road and heading to central Phoenix.

***

The driver pulled up to the gas pump at the convenience store and turned off the motor. His fists tightened on the steering wheel as he cursed. He'd been noticed and had he followed Morgan any longer, he would've been caught. He pounded his fist on the dashboard a couple times in frustration. Morgan was with the same guy from last night at her house. Who was he?

The young man chewed his lower lip, and he felt his chest tighten. In some ways, he was just like the bozo Morgan used to date. Tall, good looking, the type all girls flirted with and fell for. Nothing ever changed. Why do women do that? Don't they understand they will never be treated the way they should with these guys?

Sure, they might want to party for a while, but eventually someone new comes along and you find yourself dumped and alone. Since high school, he hoped that eventually girls would understand and appreciate that he'd always be there for them, but they never did. For the most part, they ignored him, or worse, pushed him away. But Morgan would be different. He knew it. They were destined to be together.

He glanced down at his watch. In four hours he had to be at work, but he wanted to be near her and find out how this man fit into the picture. Unfortunately, he needed this crap job. He lived in his grandmother's spare bedroom, and gave a portion of his paycheck to her to help pay for food and utilities.

He couldn't stay with his mother anymore. She was rarely at home anyway, but when she was, she often had company. He didn't like the steady stream of men.

He looked over his shoulder down Cave Creek Road. The SUV has traveled so far down the road he couldn't see it. He smiled and turned the engine back on, pulled around and headed toward the road. The small device, which sat on the passenger side of the car, had cost him a pretty penny. He'd planned to attach it to Morgan's car, but now it would go on the guy's SUV. That was a bit of a wrinkle to his plans, but no problem, he had a good idea where they were going.

CHAPTER 5

Morgan exhaled and sank back into her seat. "What made you think the driver of the economy car was my stalker?"

"Couple of things. He appeared shortly after we left your house plus the year and make of the car doesn't fit in the neighborhood."

"True," Morgan responded as she snapped the vanity mirror shut and flipped up the sun visor. "But maybe it belonged to someone who works in the area."

"You could be right." Shawn conceded.

"How much of your business is focused on bodyguard work?"

Shawn's hands tightened slightly on the steering wheel as his nerves crackled with anticipation of where Morgan's questions might lead. On the surface, her question appeared innocent enough, but the thought of tap dancing around her question made his gut tighten. He loosened his grip and exhaled slowly. "Most of the work our firm does is for events such as concerts and conventions or we work with business security. Only a small percentage is dedicated to personal protection."

He shot a quick glance over to Morgan. She had a slight smile on her lips. "Stella said you did work in the entertainment industry."

She paused and let the statement hang. Shawn focused on driving. Just as he feared, her question headed into forbidden territory. He considered how to reply. If he was too guarded, curiosity might prompt her to probe further. After a few seconds of silence he cast a quick look in her direction. "Yes. I did."

"Well?"

He turned his attention back to the road. "Well what?"

"Any names I would recognize?"

"Yeah, a few," He said.

"Who?"

Shawn glanced over. "Specifically?"

A playful laugh erupted from her. "Come on Shawn, dish. Who have you gotten up close and personal with?"

Shawn's chest tightened at her choice of words and he cleared his throat. "Honestly, I can't talk about clients. We always sign a confidentiality agreement."

"Oh."

Morgan's smile faded and she leaned back in her seat. His gut felt as if a tennis ball ricocheted around inside. He'd shut her down and disappointed her. Her feelings shouldn't matter. She was a client and when her stalker was apprehended, they'd part and he'd probably never see her again. He looked over and her brown eyes had turned serious.

"Look, I'm sorry. I really can't discuss prior assignments. Even if I could, there's not much to report. Most of the time, things are downright boring."

Morgan leaned back in her seat and began to pull out the contract from the manila envelope. "I assume there's a confidentiality agreement in here too."

Her cell phone chimed and she glanced at the number. "Brad Marshall, my ex-boyfriend."

Shawn considered ordering her to let the call go to voice-mail and yet Morgan looked at him with an expression which left no doubt that she was eager to talk to him. He wondered how long ago the breakup had taken place and what happened. If her ex was involved, talking to him wouldn't be a good idea. The phone rang two more times.

"Should I pick up?"

Shawn realized there was no delicate way to deal with this. He'd just have to lay the issue out plainly. "Do you think he is your stalker?"

Morgan shook her head. "No. The police asked the same thing yesterday. Brad didn't do this."

Morgan voice was confident when she denied her ex-boyfriend's involvement. Shawn nodded. "Okay, go ahead. But put him on speaker phone."

"What?"

He glanced over at Morgan. The stunned-deer-in-the-headlights expression said it all. "We have to be sure," he added. "I need to hear this conversation or you can let his call go to your voice mail."

For a brief second hurt flickered through her eyes, then followed with a defiant gleam. "Okay. Voice-mail," she snapped back in reply as she dropped the cell phone into her purse. "Really, this is a personal call. What makes you think you have the right to eavesdrop?"

Shawn took a slow deep breath and forced his voice to sound calm and unemotional. "You hired me to protect you until your stalker is apprehended. I can't assume someone isn't a suspect because you say they aren't. Ex-husbands and boyfriends are always top suspects in situations like this. Why are you confident he isn't involved?"

Morgan broke her gaze away from him and stared out the side window. She fidgeted with her purse and the tennis ball in his gut started ping-ponging around. He considered what he could say next but Morgan spoke first. "I know Brad isn't my stalker because he left me."

Raw pain threaded through her voice and Shawn tamped down the empathy that bubbled within in him. "I'm sorry about what happened, but if you two aren't together anymore, why would he call you?"

She shrugged. "I'm not sure. The police wanted to talk with him about yesterday. Perhaps they did."

Her answer made sense. "Can we play the message now?"

Morgan glanced over at him and didn't speak for several seconds. Finally, she sighed. "Sure. Why not?"

She brought up her voice mail and punched the speaker phone.

"Morgan. What happened yesterday? The police showed up at the office this morning to question me about your car being vandalized. Are you okay? Call me."

Morgan ended the message. "See? Does this sound like a man who'd trash my car?"

Shawn bit his tongue to censor himself from reminding her of the missing lingerie. He needed more information about Morgan's ex which meant not pissing her off any further.

"What does Brad do for a living?"

Morgan flashed him a puzzled look. "Pardon?"

"What's his profession?" Shawn asked.

"Brad's a partner at a law firm which specializes in criminal law in downtown Phoenix."

Shawn had to admit Brad might have motive, but opportunity appeared to be slim. The drive from downtown Phoenix to Scottsdale would take forty-five minutes or longer. Any absence of several hours would be noticed.

"Call him back but let him know he's on a speaker phone and I'm listening."

Morgan pressed her lips together but made no comment as she dialed the number. Seconds later, a man's voice spoke, "Morgan?"

"Hi Brad. Before you proceed, I need to inform you that you're on speaker phone and I'm in the car with my bodyguard. His name is Shawn Randall from Sonoran Security."

There was a slight pause before he spoke, as if the attorney had been caught off guard by her statement. "Morgan, what happened?"

Shawn tightened his hold on the steering wheel at the lawyer's question. The remark wasn't out of line but the fact that Morgan's ex didn't acknowledge or introduce himself to Shawn irked him.

"My car was vandalized. The police inquired about relationship issues and I reported our breakup. Brad, I told them you didn't do this," Morgan said.

"I glad to hear you say that. You can imagine my amazement when they showed up here at the office."

Shawn noted the irony in Brad's last statement. He spoke in a measured and professional tone. Not a hint of emotion, much less surprise, registered despite his words. Shawn shot a quick glance over at Morgan. She stared at the phone in her hand and appeared poised and calm but the fidgeting of her left leg told a different tale. She glanced at him and flashed a tight closed mouth smile. *She's nervous. No, hopeful.*

"Mr. Marshall, Shawn Randall here."

"Mr. Randall," the lawyer acknowledged.

"Morgan's stalker has contacted her at work and at her house. We're exploring any possible ways he gained information on her. Could one of your firm's clients be involved with this?"

"I don't think so." Brad said. "Morgan didn't make a habit of visiting our office, so the possibility of her crossing paths with any of them was small. I respectfully remind you that just because our firm deals with criminal cases you shouldn't naturally conclude that any of them would stalk Morgan."

Shawn exhaled and the sides of his lips curled in a tight forced smile. The defense attorney's experience came across loud and clear in his verbal counterpunch.

"Yes, I understand, but we must explore all angles, even remote ones," Shawn countered. "What about the firm's staff? Can you think of anyone who could be angry with Morgan or have a reason to harm her?"

Shawn braced himself. His question pushed the edge of what would be appropriate to ask. He'd deliberately asked it to provoke Morgan's ex-boyfriend and see his response.

"Mr. Randall." The lawyer's voice dripped with indignation. "I'm also concerned for Morgan's safety. However, I will not let you recklessly hurl unfounded allegations about our employees and clients. Should you choose to pursue this line of questioning further, I would suggest you first seek legal counsel."

Shawn glanced over. Shock and disbelief were written all over Morgan's face and he resisted the impulse to speak the thoughts which roared through his mind. *Get real lady. He's not coming back. This relationship was toast long before you officially broke it off.*

"I apologize. My interest is in helping find out who is stalking Morgan so we can end this trying situation and allow her to get back to her normal life. I appreciate your time and patience in this matter."

Brad's voice softened. "Morgan, I'm sorry this has happened. Please take care."

Morgan opened her mouth to reply but before she spoke, the call disconnected. She stared at the cell phone for a few seconds, before placing it back in her purse. "That cleared things up," she announced stiffly.

Shawn said nothing but chose to pretend to concentrate on the traffic. *Yeah, clear as mud.*

***

Morgan turned away and gazed out the side window in silence. How could she have put her life on hold these past few months waiting for Brad to come back? She had always clung to the hope that he'd walk into the store and apologize. He'd say how much he missed her, and that he'd been a fool to leave. What had she'd been thinking?

She cast a quick glance over at her bodyguard. His aviator-style glasses hid those all too perceptive eyes and she had no clue as to what thoughts were running through his mind. But she was certain after this conversation he pegged her as an idiot. She traced her fingers on the manila envelope that held the contract. *Thank goodness for confidentiality agreements.*

After several minutes of silence, Shawn reached down to turn on the radio when Morgan's phone rang again.

Fishing the phone out of her purse, Morgan glanced at the number. "It's Stella."

Her reflection stared back at her from shiny mirror-like eyeglass lenses. The edges of his lips tipped up slightly. "Go ahead and don't worry about the speaker phone."

She flashed a smile at him. "Thanks."

Morgan punched the call button. "Hi."

"How are things going?" Stella asked.

"Okay."

Her friend's casual tone shifted to concern. "Really? You don't sound okay."

Morgan shot a quick glance at Shawn. "Things have gotten interesting this morning and I really can't elaborate now."

Stella snorted a giggle. "He's next to you in the car, right?"

"Yes."

"How about both of you come for dinner tonight?" Stella suggested.

"Let me check." Morgan said.

She turned and gazed at Shawn as he scanned the rearview and side mirrors. "Shawn, we've been invited to dinner at Stella's tonight."

He licked his lips and inhaled while he weighed the situation. Morgan wondered if he would tell her she couldn't go. Was he concerned about the risk to Stella?

"Sure," he said.

"Stella, we're coming." Morgan confirmed on the phone. "What time?"

"Morgan, one more thing, I got a message for Stella." Shawn added.

"Wait a sec." She lowered the receiver and braced herself. What conditions would Shawn impose on her now? He shifted uncomfortably in his seat.

"Well?" Morgan asked.

He cleared his throat softly. "Tell Stella, Matt says hi."

Matt and Stella? She paused. Her friend only briefly mentioned Shawn's business partner last year when they worked together. Now it appeared like they were tentatively making an effort to connect. Morgan smirked. She brought the phone to her face. "Stella, Shawn has asked me to let you know Matt says hi."

Stella paused and then laughed softly. "Tell Shawn to let Matt know I said 'hi' back."

"Okay, will do. See you later," Morgan replied. She ended the call and returned the phone to her purse.

Shawn focused on navigating the SUV through the downtown traffic. Morgan sat back and studied him. He ignored her but shifted in his seat. His thinly veiled discomfort reminded her of an awkward schoolboy. She grinned. "Tell Matt, Stella says 'hi'. So, are you going to tell me what's going on here?"

He cast a quick glance over to her and shook his head. "Nope."

Morgan cocked her head slightly. "Sure about that?"

"I think you should ask Stella."

"Oh, I will."

***

Shawn pulled the SUV into the side entrance of the TV station's parking lot. He got out of his vehicle and surveyed the area. There wasn't anyone in sight, not even a security guard. He walked around to the passenger door to assist Morgan out of the car. As he took her hand he glanced at her face. "Are you okay?"

Morgan stared back. "I'm fine. Why did you ask?"

"Your hand is ice cold."

She forced a small tight smile. "I'm just a little nervous."

Shawn squeezed her hand. "You'll do fine. Breathe."

He reached behind her, shut the door and then gently placed his hand in the small of her back as he guided her to the entrance of the building. His fingers tingled slightly and he tamped down the urge to caress her in a half-hearted attempt to massage the tension away.

Morgan led them to the receptionist and introduced herself. Within minutes the back office entrance opened and a woman walked over to them.

"Ms. Kennedy, I'm Susan Hoffman, the producer." She turned to Shawn with an appraising gaze. "And you are?"

"This is Shawn," Morgan replied before he could speak. "He's a friend who has volunteered to drive me today."

"Okay." Susan studied him as if not convinced.

Because Morgan didn't want to introduce him in the role of a bodyguard, Shawn played along. He extended his hand out to her. "Susan, a pleasure to meet you."

"Welcome to KDEZ," she replied. "Follow me please."

Susan swiped her security badge at the door and opened it for Morgan and Shawn. Once inside she led them down a maze of hallways toward the set. Morgan stopped occasionally to study the pictures of the reporters and news anchors hanging on the wall. After she stopped for the third time, he leaned in and whispered, "Have you taped a television interview before?"

Morgan shot him a nervous look. "No. This is my first time."

Susan cleared her throat. The couple looked up to find she'd stopped and waited for them to catch up.

"Sorry," Morgan said as she scurried up to the woman.

The producer ushered them into a room which had chairs with mirrors in front of them and were lit with a large bank of lights. "Please take a seat and Liz will do your make up."

Morgan had a puzzled expression on her face but sat down without comment. Shawn stepped back and leaned on the wall behind the chair. A middle-aged woman quickly placed a light smock around Morgan's neck and reached for her makeup.

"I have make-up on," Morgan said.

"You've done a lovely job but with the bright lights you'll wash out. Don't be concerned. Even though I'm adding more you won't appear overdone in front of the camera. When you're finished, come back and I'll tone things down."

"Okay." Morgan smiled and then held still while the makeup artist applied additional blush, powder and accentuated her eyes and lips.

Shawn watched the makeup lady as she worked on Morgan and déjà vu settled in. What his client didn't know was actresses almost always arrived on set without any hairstyling or makeup on so they were a blank canvas to work on.

Over the years, he had seen stars and models considered bombshells, and without the 'Hollywood magic' most of them wouldn't get a second glance in a crowded bar on a Saturday night.

When she was done, Morgan and Shawn were guided to the set. Shawn stood behind the cameraman, scanned the surroundings, and waited. He'd never been at this station before but had been at several other ones and they all seemed alike. Space was at a premium and each square foot had a purpose. Each wall held monitors so every camera angle whether sports or weather was simply a few footsteps away. Morgan spoke and he glanced over. She'd chatted with the reporter while the camera and lighting set up was finalized. Then the interview started and within forty minutes they were walking out of the station and back to his SUV.

"Morgan, you had a great interview." Shawn said as they walked to his vehicle.

She smiled. "You think so? I've never done this before."

"I'm sure you'll be pleased when you watch it."

"Thanks."

As they approached the SUV, Shawn spied a white note stuck under the wind shield wiper on the driver's side which fluttered in the breeze. He opened the door and Morgan slid in.

"Looks like you parked in someone's space," Morgan said.

Shawn pulled the note off the windshield and glanced down. The simple blocky handwriting had a childlike quality but the message was short and to the point. *Stay away from her.*

"What the hell." He yanked his sunglasses off and surveyed the parking lot. His eyes paused and his heart skipped a beat as he spied a maroon car in the far end. He took a few steps forward and stopped when he realized the model wasn't a Honda.

"Shawn?" Morgan's voice came behind him. She'd stepped out of the vehicle and walked toward him.

"Get back in the SUV," he ordered.

"What's wrong?"

He didn't answer and continued to survey the parking lot.

"My stalker left it, right?" Morgan asked.

What should he tell her? They've been tailed and he hadn't picked up on it? His slip-up pissed him off and now he wasn't sure how Morgan would handle his reply.

"Shawn, what did the note say?"

He spun around. Morgan stood a few feet from him. "Don't you know how to follow instructions?" he growled as he strode up, grabbed her arm, and marched her back to the vehicle.

"Hey." She protested.

"In." He practically shoved her into the passenger seat. As he attempted to close the door, she stiff-armed the inside arm rest and pushed back. "He left a note for me. What did he say?"

Concern graced her face but the expression in her eyes stopped him. They say the eyes are the mirror to the soul, but he didn't believe that. Not anymore. People can fake that kind of stuff. Hell, he came from a town where people faked emotions for a living. Yet, something in her eyes mirrored strength and an inner core of resilience. When he read the letter he'd first thought she'd have a meltdown. He now knew at a gut level Morgan wasn't the meltdown type.

"At least tell me what he wants." Morgan voice possessed a calm let's-talk-about-this quality which made him question his approach in dealing with her.

Shawn ran his hand though his hair and studied the note. The sheet of paper had been torn from a spiral notebook which meant it would be almost impossible to trace.

"Shawn, hand it over."

He glanced over at Morgan. "You're wrong. The note is for me." He handed the paper to her.

She fingered the paper and her lips pressed together as she marshaled the guts to read it. After a few seconds she glanced down. She stared at the sheet for what seemed like an eternity and he studied her face, trying to guess by each subtle change in her eyes, lips, and hands what she felt. Morgan lowered her hand, still clutching the note and let out a big sigh. She leaned back into the seat and closed her eyes. "He followed us."

"Yeah, he did." He slid on his sunglasses to cut the bright summer glare and avoid direct eye contact with her. Shawn scanned the parking lot again in the vain hope if he searched one more time he'd find something he missed before. He anticipated trouble on this case but he hadn't prepared for the speed at which this had escalated.

"What do we do now?" Morgan asked. Her voice sounded soft and weary and his chest tensed as he realized she depended on him to guide her through this trial.

"We go to our next appointment," Shawn replied as he closed the car door, walked around to the driver's side, and slid into the seat.

"Shouldn't we call the police?"

He sifted through the keys on his keychain and then glanced over at Morgan. "And report what? Our suspicions about a burgundy Honda driver with no license plate number?" Morgan stared at him in silence for a few seconds. "I told you this would get worse. Here it goes."

Morgan eyes watered. "I don't understand. Why me?"

Shawn put the key in the ignition and started the engine. "I don't know, but we'll stop him, I promise."

Morgan slouched back in the seat and nervously scanned the parking lot as they left.

"On to the resort?" he asked. Morgan nodded as she stared down at the note.

Shawn used the quiet time while he drove the SUV to the resort to think. Morgan's stalker was behaving like a jealous lover. Brad hadn't mentioned receiving any threats so Morgan's stalker knew they'd broken up. He tightened his grip on the steering wheel, checked all the side and rearview mirrors and assessed the cars around them in traffic. Satisfied they weren't followed, he shot a quick glance over at Morgan. She appeared lost in thought as she stared out the passenger side window.

He pressed his lips together and focused on driving. He'd lied to her. Shawn knew why this man had singled Morgan out. Besides good looks, she possessed an appeal which came from strength and kindness. She was approachable. A quality which drew her stalker to her like a moth to a flame. And, for what it was worth, he would be willing to bet a steak dinner that they'd been watched at Morgan's house last night.

CHAPTER 6

Matt stepped out of his car, pushed his sunglasses up the bridge of his nose and waited as a family of quail scurried across to the far end of the driveway to the desert bushes. He surveyed Morgan's property and shook his head. "Wide open desert," he murmured. "Ms. Kennedy, you've got a problem."

He walked the perimeter of her house. The first recommendation: add exterior lights attached to motion detectors. Anyone sneaking around outside would think twice about trying to get in when the lights flashed on.

The sound of voices in the distance caught his attention. Two riders on horseback made their way down the dry wash along Morgan's property line. They disappeared as they passed behind the brush. *If I'd wanted to spy on Morgan that's where I'd hide.* Matt returned to his notes and, when he finished, he walked over the back of the property and stepped down into the wash.

To the east he could see the riders in the distance. To the west he spied the brush and the ironwood tree that the riders disappeared behind earlier. Matt trekked up the wash through the loose sand and silt until he reached the spot. Years of sporadic flooding eroded away the soil making the depth of the wash deeper by the tree. He maneuvered around the tree and discovered what he was searching for, a perfect line of sight to Morgan's arcadia door. He moved closer to the bushes and nudged around them with his foot. A flash of light hit something. He gently pulled the scrub back and spied an empty water bottle. "Jackpot," he whispered.

He slid his pen into the bottle's open mouth and extracted it from the bush. A fine thin layer of dust coated the plastic surface. "Were you careless and held the bottle with your bare hands?" Matt whispered.

Once back at his car, he opened his trunk, pulled a plastic evidence bag out, and dropped the bottle inside. He then tossed the bag and the notebook on the front passenger seat and dialed Shawn's number.

When Shawn answered, he began, "Access to the house is way too easy. Do you think she'd be willing to add a fence?"

"Not sure, but you can ask when we come to the office later."

"Problems?"

"You could say that," Shawn replied before he updated Matt on the happenings this morning. Shawn kept his voice light and matter-of-fact which meant one thing: Morgan could hear Shawn's comments.

"Hey, you know what they say, persistence is a virtue," Matt joked.

Shawn snorted a half laugh. "As with most things, even virtues aren't good when taken to extremes."

"If the fence is a no go, I'm recommending she install some motion sensors and have them attached to spot lights set to turn on if anyone approaches her house."

"Okay, anything else?"

"Yeah, I think our boy has been watching her at home," Matt said. "I've found an empty water bottle. I'll send it to Scottsdale P.D. Maybe they'll find prints on them. What did the note on your SUV say?"

"Just your basic threat, stay away or else."

"A man of few words," Matt responded. "Let me make a couple phone calls. The station must have security cameras. Maybe we'll get a look at this guy. Where are you going next?"

"We're heading over to Copper Creek Inn and then back to the store. I'll be stopping by the office on the way back; I need to pick up something."

Matt paused as a small adrenaline surge jolted through him. "Your gun?"

"Yep."

Matt pressed his lips together and inhaled deeply. He searched for the words to the next question. Shawn had a license to carry a concealed weapon. In fact, Matt did too. But neither made a habit of carrying guns on a regular basis. "Is Ms. Kennedy prepared for this?" Matt asked.

Shawn didn't respond immediately. "Let's discuss this when we come in to the office later."

Matt exhaled with a soft chuckle. "Okay, partner. I'll see if we can get KDEZ's security camera footage. I'll give you a call when I have something."

"Thanks"

***

On the trip to Copper Creek Inn, Morgan contemplated how much her life had changed within the past twenty-four hours. By this time yesterday she discovered a man, whom she'd never met, had succeeded in making her life a living hell.

Before this, simple activities such as answering her phone and coming and going where she pleased would've never taken place under the protection of a bodyguard. She couldn't decide which was worse, the frustration or the fear.

The phone call this morning with Brad had been a serious wakeup call. She'd been confident if she gave him space, he'd come back to her. Instead, he'd moved on.

She replayed the last few times they were together through her mind, and now she saw the clear signals he'd given her. Late for dates, last-minute cancels, and the last time they went out for dinner, she caught his eyes traveling around the room, checking out other women. She closed her eyes and leaned back into the seat. The warning signs had been there all the time and yet, she'd ignored them. There'd been no fights, no scenes toward the end, just a slow drift away from each other.

When did it happen? Memories played through her mind like the rewind function on a DVR. Then she knew. It started after "the talk." Over drinks one night Morgan told him that she wanted to settle down and start a family. She chalked the glazed over look on

Brad's face to an alcohol buzz. But it wasn't. Deep down she knew the end of their relationship had arrived.

Had there been any signs she was being stalked? Did she ignore those too? She opened her eyes and looked out the front windshield. Had she seen him around and discounted it? Did she know who he was?

Needle pricks stung her eyes and she closed them in an effort to fight off the tears which threatened to spill. She wouldn't cry. Not here, not with Shawn sitting next to her.

She glanced over at Shawn while he was focused on driving. He sat straight in the seat with a firm grip on the wheel. Even with his aviator glasses, the precise moves of his head indicated he was scanning the side and rear view mirrors. What did he know that she didn't?

"Would you mind if we turned on the radio?" Shawn asked.

Morgan glanced away and looked out the side window. "Sure, go ahead."

Shawn reached over and punched the button. A soft ballad came on and she saw the station number on the radio screen. Strange, her first impulse would've been to peg him as a sports station or rock-and-roll listener.

"Is this okay? Do you want to change the station?"

"No, it's fine."

The lunch-hour traffic slowed their exit from downtown and she relaxed as the music continued. Her empty stomach growled, demanding food.

"Do you want to stop and get something to eat?" Shawn asked.

Morgan placed her hand over her stomach, realizing he must've heard the rumble. "Not right now. Let's get something when we get to the resort. With all that's going on, I don't think I can handle greasy fast food today."

He shrugged. "Your call."

Morgan felt a slight twinge of guilt at his reply. She never thought to ask if he wanted to stop and eat. "We can stop if you want," she added hastily.

"No, I'm good."

***

Shawn focused on the driving and tried to ignore the awkward silence filling the cab. Morgan underwent a total change from this morning after the note was left. The fun easy-going woman had retreated into silence, thinking only God knows what. It didn't take a psychic to see stress rolling off her like steam.

Please, spare me from a woman who never eats, he prayed silently. It was an epidemic among the women he dated in California. No matter where he took them, they all pushed their food around their plates, fearful one bite would spiral into some shark-like feeding frenzy.

He glanced over at her and made a silent vow that once the business was finished at the resort, they would take a lunch break. The last thing he needed right now was a client collapsing from a combination of low blood sugar and heat.

Thirty minutes later, Shawn drove through the manicured entrance of the resort and slowly snaked along the curved driveway toward the hotel's main building. He marveled at how well the resort balanced its seventy-year-old history with contemporary luxury. Nestled at the base of Mummy Mountain, the adobe building, which served as the main entrance and lobby, retained its traditional southwestern architecture. Once inside, guests were surrounded by expensive Western and Native American art any museum would've been proud to showcase. He had to admit, the location was an impeccable choice to hold a high dollar charity fundraiser.

Shawn pulled into a nearby parking lot and drove around. *No burgundy Honda.* Satisfied, he pulled into a space. Given recent activity, he preferred not to use valet parking because that meant handing his keys to a stranger who parked his SUV in some out-of-the-way lot. He'd had enough surprises for today.

He went around to the passenger side of the car, helped Morgan out, and escorted her to the resort's front entrance. Upon entering the lobby, Morgan led them to the event planner's offices.

"Ellen, are you ready?" Morgan asked.

The short petite woman stood up from behind her desk and came over to greet them. "Yes, Ms. Kennedy. Please follow me."

Morgan smiled in approval and introduced Shawn as a security specialist. If Ellen thought anything was out of place, Shawn couldn't tell as the woman smiled graciously and extended her hand. "Mr. Randall."

He'd have to give it to Morgan. Her introduction as a security specialist was a nice touch. Not the complete truth, but not a lie either.

"If you will follow me down to the Arizona Ballroom, they're setting up the tables and chairs at this time." Morgan nodded and they followed Mary out and across the outside entrance to the wing where the conference and meeting rooms were located.

The tables were arranged in clusters with a clear path up the front where a podium and empty display cases waited to be positioned. Morgan spent a few minutes in discussion on layout, making some minor revisions, confirming timelines for dinner service and arrival of the jewelry.

He couldn't help but admire her while she reviewed the plans. Morgan was in her element. Always pleasantly clear in her instructions and the changes she requested, Morgan demonstrated her knowledge and experience with this type of project. When finished, she glanced over at him and smiled. She's relaxed, he thought.

"Shawn, do you like Mexican food?" Morgan asked.

"Love it. Where do you want to go?"

Ellen interjected, "Lupe's is off the swimming pool terrace and the food is wonderful. Please be our guest."

Morgan grinned. "What do you think?"

"I'm game if you are."

Morgan turned back to the hotel representative. "I think we'll take you up on your offer."

"Wonderful," Ellen replied. "Please follow me."

The event planner chatted briefly with Morgan as she escorted them to the restaurant. Shawn scanned the dining room when they arrived. The restaurant's décor had a more contemporary touch than the lobby. Leather chairs and Native American sculptures complemented the earth tones and sleek copper accents. As they settled into their chairs and surveyed the menus he asked, "Dine here often?"

"No," Morgan replied. "I haven't been here for ages."

He grinned and shook his head. "Too bad, I'm depending upon your recommendation on what to order."

Morgan grinned. "The food was wonderful the last time I was here. Anything you choose will be great. Just be warned, the portions are huge."

After they placed their orders, Morgan took a sip from her iced tea. "How did you start with the security business?"

Shawn's stomach gave a sharp twinge at her question. He fiddled with his knife to collect his thoughts before responding. He had to be careful. Certain topics he couldn't discuss and Morgan's innocent questions could detour into forbidden territory.

"I started when I got off the LAPD about five years ago. I first worked for an agency that specialized in security work for the entertainment industry."

"Sounds interesting. Why did you come to Arizona?"

Shawn stopped fingering the knife and studied her. Morgan had managed to get to the heart of what he couldn't discuss in two short questions. He set the knife down, reached for his iced tea, and took a sip. *Time to take a page from her playbook. Tell her the truth, but not all of it.* "I needed a change and decided to leave the LA scene to start my own business. So, I came here."

The waiter arrived with their meals and gave Shawn a reprieve. They ate in silence for several minutes, but just as Shawn began to believe he was out of the woods, Morgan asked, "So where did you meet Matt?"

Safe question, easy answer, he thought. "Matt worked for the same agency I did. When I decided to start a new agency in Phoenix, he wanted in on the ground floor and came along."

"Does he work for you?"

"No, he's my partner. He has expertise in electronic surveillance and security systems. In fact, he's assembled quite a team for the installation of security systems for businesses.

"Is he married?"

Shawn, who had been ready to take a bite of his burger, threw her a glance. She had a curious expression, leaving no doubt she'd picked up on the mutual interest between Matt and Stella. He suppressed a grin. If offering up his partner's love life would keep her out of his, he'd be happy to oblige.

"No," he replied. "Matt dates off and on. No serious relationships, as far as I know."

Morgan smiled and took another bite of her salad. "What did he recommend for my house?"

"Matt doesn't like the fact that the whole property is open to the desert. Anyone could walk up to your house with nothing to stop them. Would you consider building a fence?"

"Not unless I had no choice. I love the view at sunset and the wildlife. I had a family of javelina travel through my backyard a couple weeks back." Morgan paused and her expression darkened. "Do I have a choice?"

"I'm not sure," Shawn said. "This situation with your stalker could resolve itself quickly or it could take a while."

Morgan glanced down at her salad and pushed the greens around with her fork. Shawn could see that she had questions but didn't want to spill any more information about California. "I have a loft over by Kierland Commons. It's got a nice view of the mountains to the north, but no wildlife." -

She looked up at him. "Give me a few days to decide about the fence."

"Sure."

Morgan's request made sense. They may have a better feel about how things might play out in a few days anyway. Shawn's cell phone vibrated. He reached down and looked at the number. "The office," he announced before he answered.

"Good news," Matt announced. "KDEZ has a security camera on the parking lot. I sent Sabrina down to pick up a copy of the footage. We should be able to see who put the note on your SUV."

Shawn exhaled in relief. Finally, a break. "Great. We're finishing lunch and will come straight in."

Morgan placed her napkin on the table and bent over to reach for her purse. "In fact, we're on our way now."

Morgan picked up her purse, removed some money for the tip, and pushed her chair away from the table. On the way out, she specifically stopped to thank the restaurant manager.

Shawn took her arm as they weaved around the people and their luggage on the way through the lobby. He thought they had almost cleared the area when a young child who had been playing, knocked over a small pile of suitcases. The luggage slammed into Morgan's leg and she toppled into him. Without thinking, Shawn wrapped his arm around her waist to steady her. She glanced up and flashed an embarrassed grin. As she regained her balance, her hair brushed against his jaw and he caught a slight scent of lavender. He swore he could hear the pounding of his heart and loosened his grip slightly. "Are you okay?"

"Fine," Morgan replied. "I didn't wear the right shoes for the obstacle course today."

Shawn smirked. "Yeah, who would have thought you'd need track shoes." He exhaled slightly and released his hold as she steadied herself. For a fleeting second he became keenly aware that his arms were empty and he consciously dropped them.

Shawn turned his gaze to the young boy who started the avalanche. He stood off to the right, frozen in slack-jawed amazement. "Sam." A woman's voice barked. A young blonde woman walked up and grabbed her son's hand. She turned to Shawn and Morgan. "I'm so sorry."

Morgan smiled. "No harm done."

"We're okay." Shawn said.

"Here, let me help." A bellman stepped over, began to stack the suitcases, and once a clear path had opened, Shawn placed his hand in the small of Morgan's back and urged her forward out of the entrance.

Once outside, they picked up their pace as they walked to his vehicle. Shawn scanned the parking lot looking for anything suspicious. Anxiety edged his gut as he checked the gaps between the parked cars as they passed by them. He couldn't shake the feeling that they were being watched. He glanced back at the front entrance. Nothing appeared out of place. A car had pulled up to the covered entrance and the bellman from the lobby arrived with a cart to unload the trunk. For a brief moment, the uniformed employee glanced over at them before focusing on unloading the luggage.

As they approached his SUV, another piece of paper stuck under his windshield wiper.

"Dear God, please, not another note." Morgan murmured.

Shawn didn't comment. He gripped her arm and he steered her to the passenger side. After he opened the door, Morgan slid into the seat, but before he could close the door she let out an anguished gasp and pointed to a small mass on hood.

Adrenaline coursed through him as if fuel injected. He glanced over at Morgan. Despite the heat, her face was drained of color. I've got to hold this together for her sake, he thought.

Shawn closed the door, stepped around the front of the SUV and cautiously approached the driver's side. He recognized it, a dead rabbit. *The son-of-a-bitch had placed road kill on his vehicle.* The blood was still wet and the few organs that peeped through the fur were still moist. Taking the note off the windshield, he read it. "You're next."

Shawn folded the note and placed it in his jacket pocket before he went to the back of the SUV and opened up the tailgate. He reached into the metal box in the back, pulled out a pair of disposable vinyl gloves, and donned them. He'd seen much worse in his days on the LAPD but his stomach still tightened and churned as he gently lifted the rabbit from the windshield. He set it in a trash receptacle a few feet down from his vehicle, removed the gloves carefully so as to not touch the external surface, and dropped them inside.

By the time he returned to the driver's door, Morgan sat in silence and stared at the mountains in the distance. "This has got to stop."

"It will," he replied.

"When?" Morgan snapped. "I have a fundraiser at the end of the week. I can't go into hiding. Too much depends on this. Do you have any idea what this is like? Have you ever been in my shoes?"

Shawn looked at her. Her cheeks were flushed with anger and her eyes had a fierce edge to them. Textbook response, he thought grimly. First shock, next denial, now anger.

"No Morgan, I haven't."

She glared at him as she took deep rapid breaths and looked like an Amazon warrior ready for battle.

Shawn looked down and studied his keys in stoic silence. She was right. He had handled situations like this several times, but he had never been in her place. He'd never been the object of a stalker.

"I don't know what it is like to be in your shoes. I'm sorry if I've come across as unsympathetic, but-"

Before he could finish Morgan interrupted him. "Shawn, no, I'm sorry." She paused and took a deep breath. "I shouldn't have lost my temper with you."

"Whoa." Shawn's head snapped up. In all the years he had been in the security business, he could count on one hand the number of times a client had apologized after dumping all over the security team. Miss Morgan Kennedy had managed to do what rock stars and movie idols had never done, seriously impress him.

"No problem," he replied quietly as he slipped the key in the ignition and started the engine. "Now, let's go to my office and get a look at the security footage," he growled.

CHAPTER 7

How could I have snapped at him? Morgan slumped into the seat and stared out the front window. In all the years she'd worked at the store, she'd never lost her cool with a customer or employee, but this whole situation with the stalker had rattled her so badly she had practically bitten Shawn's head off.

Morgan studied Shawn as he drove. At first glance, you'd think he was calm but she picked up little details that told a different story. He sat ramrod straight, and his grip on the steering wheel was firm, so much so that his knuckles were white, literally. His head moved in small precise movements, and his eyes searched the review and side mirrors more often than if this had been a casual drive. He was on full scale alert.

"What did the note say?" She asked.

Shawn glanced over to her and then returned his gaze to the road. "You're next."

"You're next?"

"Yeah."

The meaning sank in, and she swallowed as her throat and chest tightened. *Now he's in danger too because of me.* The overwhelming urge to move, run and get away from all of this hit her. She raked her fingers through her hair, closed her eyes and laid her head against the back of the seat. She uttered a silent prayer. *Come on Shawn, say something. Tell me that things are going to turn out fine. Say you've seen this before and we'll catch the stalker and my life will return to normal.*

"I think you should know that when I leave the office this afternoon I will be upgrading my Taser to a gun," Shawn said.

Morgan gulped, *So much for silent prayers and wishful thinking.* "Is this necessary?"

Shawn nodded. "I expect him to try something soon."

His words from last night echoed through her mind, *we're not dealing with a normal person here.* She turned and gazed out the side window. She had too many questions and no answers.

Shawn pulled the SUV into a parking lot outside of an office building located at the Scottsdale Airpark.

"We're here," he said as he turned off the ignition.

She surveyed a cube of steel and tinted glass. Nothing distinctive or unusual about it, there had to be hundreds of buildings which looked like it in the metro area.

"It's perfect for our needs, close to the freeway, and not too high profile," Shawn said. She nodded and wondered if he had read her thoughts.

As they walked through the front doors of the lobby, a cool blast of air-conditioned air hit them, and Morgan sucked in a deep breath and stopped at the elevator. Shawn turned and beckoned her on. "No, we're on the first floor, this way."

He guided her to a second set of doors. He held the door open for her to step through.

Bright sunlight blinded her momentarily, and her eyes slammed shut. She peered through squinted lids seconds later and spied lush vegetation as the sound of babbling water greeted her. Somewhere among the densely landscaped courtyard was a waterfall. Shawn stepped away from her side and led her down the sidewalk.

Office doors on her right were spaced like dominos every twenty to thirty yards. All of them had an office number on them, but only a few had a business name posted and she wondered what other types of businesses were tucked away around here. Shawn stopped and opened the door to suite one hundred and seventeen. Morgan stepped through the door. Given the size of the front office, Shawn's business didn't get much walk-in traffic. A woman with brown hair behind the reception desk smiled at her.

"Morgan, this is Laura."

"Hello." Morgan said.

"Can I get you something, bottled water perhaps?" The receptionist asked.

"Thank you."

"Laura, please bring it to my office. Is Matt in?"

"Yes," Laura replied.

Shawn ushered Morgan through the door to the right of the front desk and escorted her down the hallway. If the television station had a nonstop gallery of photos and posters, Sonoran Security was on the other end of the spectrum. The walls were barren of any photos, and the gray industrial carpeting lent an un-inhabited air about the office. "How long have you been here?" Morgan asked.

"Three years." He opened a side door and switched on the light. "Have a seat. I'll be back." He turned and left, closing the door behind him.

Morgan sighed and looked around the office. The knot between her shoulders began to unwind and with each successive breath, the nervous edge washed away as she surveyed the room.

A dark cherry wood desk faced the door and a matching credenza sat against the wall. A few papers were stacked in neat piles on his desk, but the gallery of photos on the wall behind it captured her attention.

She moved closer and inspected them. A police academy photo hung on the far left. She searched a bit before she located Shawn. The next five autographed pictures featured rock bands and singers. The impressive collection of photos forced her to conclude that despite the long hours and stress, the personal security business came with some cool perks.

The next picture had been taken on a movie set. Shawn smiled at the camera, his arm draped over the shoulders of a slender actress who wore a costume straight out of the Old West. Morgan leaned in and recognized the woman, Christy Thomas. She had her arm wrapped around Shawn's waist, and she smiled up at him. Shawn's eyes sparkled with amusement, as if they shared some inside joke, and the picture oozed with an intimacy all the other pictures lacked.

The last few photos featured a few movie and television celeb-rities and one of Shawn in the background of a red carpet premiere.

But the image of Shawn and Christy drew Morgan back. What was the story behind the picture?

She glanced at a framed photograph on the credenza of a small girl. Morgan estimated her to be two or three years old. The toddler snuggled in Shawn's arms with her head against his chest and her tiny arms stretched upward almost curling around his neck. Shawn gazed back in the camera with an expression Morgan couldn't quite fathom. He appeared comfortable holding the child, but his eyes possessed an edge of wariness.

The next photo featured the same child. She appeared a few years older. She had a large smile with a gap where her front tooth had fallen out. The final picture contained Shawn, Christy and the girl.

She scanned the photos again and returned to the last one. It reminded her of a family photo. She studied the girl more closely. *Same eye and hair color as Shawn's. Could this child be his daughter?* "Stop it. I'm being silly," she whispered as she stepped back from the wall.

But Morgan's mind hung onto the thought like a bulldog, and she tried to recall if she had ever heard about Christy Thomas having a young child. She never followed the Hollywood tabloids, so what little she knew about Christy Thomas was skeletal at best. The lady kept a low profile between movies.

The door opened behind Morgan, and she spun around. Laura entered and handed her the bottled water.

"Here you go. Quite a collection of photos, don't you think?"

"Yes," Morgan replied. She flashed the receptionist a quick smile. For some strange reason, she felt a little like a child whose hand had been caught in the cookie jar. Morgan itched to inquire about the not-so-famous face of the young girl in the photo gallery, but couldn't figure out what to say without sounding like some kind of paparazzi-style stalker.

"If I can get you anything else, please don't hesitate to ask." Laura said as she left and closed the door behind her.

Morgan sat down on the chair in front of the desk and took a small sip of water while she processed what she'd seen. Were Shawn and Christy married? He gave no hint of this earlier when they talked at lunch, and he didn't sport a wedding ring. Of course, that didn't mean anything, Morgan knew from years of working in the jewelry store that a high percentage of men opted not to wear a ring. She stared at the photos as if the answer would come to her. Shawn had up close and personal access on sets, so a romance was possible. She had to admit having to depend upon a bodyguard for protection fit into the knight-in-shining-armor storyline quite well too. What did she know about him, really? The door opened, and she turned to see Shawn enter followed by a tall, lanky, sandy-haired man.

"Morgan, this is my partner, Matt Anderson."

"Ms. Kennedy." The man extended his hand and shook hers. Morgan tried not to be obvious while she studied him. A trace of an accent hinted he came from somewhere in the South. His face had a rugged angular look which reminded her of an action hero, but his sharp jaw line ended with a dimple on his chin. A feature, Morgan decided, which added a boyish aspect to him. No wonder Stella seemed interested.

Matt sat next to her while Shawn walked around and took the chair behind his desk.

Matt spoke first. "Shawn recapped what happened today, and I'd like to talk about what I discovered at your house."

Morgan waited for him to continue.

"From a security standpoint, your home provides some challenges. The property is not fenced, and access is too easy. The quick fix is to add security lighting with motion detectors attached, which should discourage uninvited guests. Now, I don't want to scare you, but when I walked the wash behind your property, I found a water bottle dumped in the brush by the ironwood tree. I suspect someone has been watching you."

A chill seeped into her and she sat back in the chair. No wonder Shawn asked if she'd consider adding a fence today at lunch. She took another sip of water. "Couldn't the bottle have been left by hikers or a horseback rider?"

"Perhaps," Matt said. "I'd like to send it to the Scottsdale PD. Maybe they'll get some fingerprints and see if they match anything on your car. Do you have the name of the officer who came out to the store yesterday?"

"Yes." Morgan reached for her purse and fished out the business card for Officer Romano.

"There's more," Shawn said.

Morgan peered at Shawn and then back to Matt. Both men had the same worried expression on their faces. "What else?"

"Things have deteriorated at a rapid pace," Shawn added. He paused and Morgan watched him struggle with what to say next.

"In the last twenty-four hours there has been one act of vandalism and two threats. Your stalker is desperate, and we're concerned he may hurt you or someone around you."

Morgan glanced at Matt. He nodded in agreement.

Shawn continued, "We think you shouldn't spend any time at your home while this guy is stalking you."

Morgan's stomach tightened. "Go into hiding? I won't do that. With the fundraiser, the store, and considering my father's health, I can't expect him to step up and run this."

"I'm not suggesting you drop off the radar. Just not be at your home alone," Shawn said.

Morgan paused. "Okay, what do you recommend?"

Shawn looked over at Matt who returned a knowing glance. He took a deep breath and exhaled. "I live in a high-rise condo with restricted access. We think," and he nodded over at Matt, "that you should move into the spare bedroom until we get this cleared up."

Move in with Shawn? The idea appealed and unnerved her at the same time. If he was involved with Christy Thomas, how would staying at his place go over with her? If Morgan were in Christy's shoes, the answer would be not too well. "What if I stayed with my parents?"

Shawn shook his head. "Not a good idea. He has threatened me for being with you. I believe this guy is quite capable of following up on those threats. You'll put your parents in danger too."

"I have to agree with Shawn." Matt added.

Morgan sighed. She couldn't put her parents in harm's way. "Just for the record, having a stalker completely..." She paused, searching for a word to finish the sentence.

"Sucks," Shawn said.

Morgan forced a small smile and nodded. "Yeah, that's the word."

"Oh, wait until you taste Shawn's cooking," Matt cracked.

Morgan smiled at his attempt to lighten the situation. A soft rap on the door interrupted.

"Yes," Shawn answered.

The door opened, and a petite young woman with long dark hair looked at Matt and then Shawn. "I have the security footage."

"Great," Matt replied as he stood up. "Morgan, I'd like to introduce you to Sabrina. She's part of the technical support team."

The woman shifted her glance from Matt to Morgan. "Hello."

Matt spoke, "Let's go to the conference room, where we can review the footage on the big screen." Sabrina nodded and left. By the time Morgan, Shawn, and Matt arrived, Sabrina had already turned on the power to the TV and inserted the DVD into the player.

"This covers a four hour period from eight to noon. We should have footage of you and whoever left the note," Sabrina said.

Matt gestured for Morgan to sit. Shawn sat next to her and Matt sank into a chair on the other side of the table closest to the screen.

"Let's take a look," Shawn said.

Sabrina fast forwarded through the footage. "You arrived around ten-thirty, right?"

"Close enough," Shawn replied.

For the next couple minutes, everyone in the room watched cars and people move in what could best be described as warp drive. Finally Shawn's SUV pulled into the parking lot. Sabrina stopped, backed up, and set the player on normal speed.

Shawn stepped out of his vehicle. The camera had been positioned on the roof, and must've been at least one hundred feet away. Morgan couldn't make out much detail as Shawn walked around to her on the passenger side of the vehicle.

"We're not going to get a close up of the guy's face," Shawn commented.

"Nope," Matt replied.

Everyone waited as video played on. Finally, after about ten minutes, a car pulled up. Morgan held her breath while Shawn and Matt leaned forward in their seats as if getting closer to the TV screen would give them a better view.

A young man stepped out of his car, looked around, and then walked up to their vehicle. Morgan pressed her lips together as she nervously rocked her foot. He was tall, dark-haired, and had a slender build. Nothing about him was distinctive. She had hoped for so much more from the security footage.

He walked over to the SUV, anchored the note under the windshield wiper, then squatted down on the driver's side and reached inside the wheel well.

"What's he doing?" Morgan asked.

Neither Shawn nor Matt responded as the footage continued. Within seconds, the man got back into his car and drove off. Sabrina turned on the lights. Both men stood up in unison and strode out of the room. Morgan and Sabrina followed, practically having to jog to keep up with them as they raced to Shawn's SUV.

By the time Morgan reached the vehicle, she found Matt squatting by the driver's side and reaching up inside. His face was emotionless as he moved his arm around and searched. Then he crooked a grin, "Gotcha." He stood up and held something up for them to see.

"What is it?" Morgan asked.

"A tracking device," Sabrina answered.

"That explains a lot," Shawn added.

Matt tossed the device to Shawn. "Yeah, you weren't followed to the resort, you were tracked."

CHAPTER 8

"I was right, we weren't followed." Shawn muttered as he studied the tracking device in his hand. After sighting the Honda this morning, he hadn't noticed anything the rest of the day. The second note and the road kill rabbit had thrown him, and made him question if he'd lost his touch. Shawn glanced up at his partner and Matt's furrowed brow made him pause.

"What?" Shawn asked.

"I don't know. This stalker has talent. I've never run across one who's placed electronic equipment on a vehicle before," Matt said.

"Do you think he's tampered with anything else?"

"No. To do something like that would take more time and a bit of privacy. The video showed he hit and ran. But now that we know what we are up against, I can make sure he can't track you."

Shawn asked. "How?"

"Simple. These tracking devices are available at a number of places. The primary clientele is the suspicious wife or husband who tracks the comings and goings of their spouses."

"So?"

"Well, these companies also offer a countermeasure. You plug the device into your cigarette lighter to jam the tracking device. There's one in our storage room."

Sabrina piped up. "I'll get it."

"Thanks." Matt replied.

Shawn glanced at Morgan. Her arms crossed her body, and her firmly pressed lips melted into a frown as she stared at the device he held in his hand.

"I don't believe this. Electronic tracking devices and countermeasures, I'm beginning to think I'm in a James Bond movie. What's next?"

"Weaponry," Shawn said.

Morgan threaded her fingers through her hair and shot him a nervous expression before looking away. Shawn swallowed. He'd seen this reaction before. Morgan had reached the point which signaled the dying gasp of denial. The stage where a client grasped and completely understood the danger they were in. *Goodbye denial, hello fear.*

"Do you have an issue with me carrying a gun?" he asked.

"Yes. No." Morgan shrugged, "Sort of."

"Why?"

She stared at him and sighed. "I don't know why. But I'm uncomfortable. Don't get me wrong. We use armored trucks to pick up large deposits and to transport jewelry but..." She paused as she gazed off at the bank of storm clouds developing on the horizon.

"I realize you're trained and licensed to carry a firearm. Still, something could go wrong and a gun is deadly force."

Shawn tamped down his frustration.

"Hey, why don't we take this discussion indoors? Morgan will be safer, and everyone will be a lot cooler," Matt suggested.

Shawn nodded, and they walked back to the office.

"When do you have to return to the store?" Matt asked.

"Four," Morgan answered.

Shawn glanced down at his wristwatch. They had ten to fifteen minutes before they'd have to leave and he knew convincing Morgan that carrying a side arm is a good idea would take more time.

As they walked in the reception area, Morgan asked Laura, "Where's your restrooms?"

"Down the hall, first door on the left," The receptionist replied.

"I'll be in my office," Shawn said.

Morgan nodded and continued down the hallway. Once she disappeared, Shawn strode to his office and closed the door behind him. He unlocked his desk drawer and pulled out his holster, shed his jacket, and armed himself. He'd barely slid the jacket on when Matt came into the room.

"Here you go." Matt handed over the jamming device.

"Thanks. Everything set for Friday's concert?"

"We're good. Don't worry. Focus on Morgan and call me if you need any more assistance."

Shawn nodded. "I've got things under control."

Matt slanted a glance his way. "You think so?"

He regarded his partner's all-too-knowing air. "What?"

Matt smirked.

"Hell, I know that look. Speak up."

"What do you think about her?" His partner asked.

Shawn shrugged and feigned nonchalance. "What's not to like? She's young, pretty, smart, and rich, the total package."

Matt arched his brows, creating an expression of tolerant disbelief.

He avoided his friend's gaze and closed the desk drawer. "It shows, doesn't it?"

"A little," his partner replied.

Shawn shook his head and glared at his partner. "The last thing I need is to get involved with a client. You know what happened in L.A."

His partner glanced at the photo of the child on the credenza behind his desk. "She isn't Christy."

"Thank God for small miracles. One Christy is quite enough," Shawn growled.

Matt started to reply, but stopped when someone knocked on the door.

"Come in," Shawn said.

Morgan stood at the entrance. "We need to leave now if we're going to be there on time."

"I'm ready." Shawn walked around the desk and threw his partner a quick glance. "When you hear back on the water bottle, please call me."

***

The silence on the drive to the store made the twenty minutes feel like forty. Morgan spotted the gun under Shawn's jacket when she got into the vehicle, and realized he'd disregarded her concerns.

She didn't hold an irrational fear of guns. Shawn probably thought she was one of those people who believed no one ever needed to carry a gun. But the fact that he felt it necessary to arm himself terrified her. What did Shawn expect to happen? She glanced over and studied him. His posture had softened a bit, yet he continually scanned the windows and mirrors, hunting, always on alert and searching.

When they reached the shopping mall, Morgan pointed to the turn off which lead to the parking behind the row of buildings. "We can park behind the store and go to the back entrance."

Shawn slowly turned the opposite direction and moved down the first row of parking spaces. "No. There's too much privacy behind the store. Lots of foot traffic and people who might observe something is the prescription we need right now."

He reached the end of the row and turned right into the adjoining path. After Shawn passed on the second available space, Morgan realized he wasn't searching for a place to park, but instead was patrolling the lot. Only when he had checked out the whole area did he double back and park near the jewelry store.

As they walked in the front entrance, Mary glanced up from the counter. "How did the interview go?"

"Fine," Morgan replied. "Are they here?"

"They're in your office."

A twinge of anxiety pinged through her. Morgan hadn't told her dad about the stalker. She'd hoped to spare him this element of stress. Now, she'd have to explain what happened to her car and why she had a six foot two-inch man shadowing her twenty-four seven.

Shawn came up beside her as she punched the security code to the back area. "Does your father know about this?"

She glanced at him and tried to crook a smile his way. "He will soon."

Morgan took a few strides through the work area and then turned around. Shawn had stopped to survey the tables and equipment. "You design and create jewelry?"

"Sometimes for special customers or events, we'll order gems and design custom pieces."

"Who's the designer?"

Morgan smiled. His serious expression had melted into a curious boyish charm. "Well, since you asked."

She walked up to Shawn and rose up on her toes and leaned in close enough to whisper in his ear. "The owner's daughter, she designs pieces and makes them."

Morgan settled down on her heels and moved back a half step. Shawn's lips curved up in a smile. "Vicki?"

Morgan laughed and gave him a playful punch. "No, I've designed for years."

"I'd like you to show me some of them."

Morgan held her breath. A flirtatious twinkle lit his eyes as he looked at her. Here it was. The connection she sensed briefly when they first met. The little voice in her head warned her to be careful because he wasn't available. Morgan took another step back and cleared her throat. "Uh, let's do that after the meeting and not keep my father waiting any longer."

"Lead the way." Shawn gestured toward the offices in the corner.

She paused briefly at her office door and glanced back at him. "Here goes," she muttered as she turned the doorknob and entered the office, "Dad."

William Kennedy stood up and embraced his daughter. "How's my girl?" Morgan started to reply, but he glanced over at Shawn. "Who are you?"

"Dad, we need to talk." She turned to the web designer. "Could you give us a few minutes, please?"

The jean-clad man looked at the trio. "No problem. I'll be out on the sales floor." After he left, Shawn stepped in and shut the door.

Morgan took a breath and for a second she swore she could hear her heart beating in the silence. With the three of them in the space, her office seemed small. "Dad, this is Shawn Randall. He is the owner of Sonoran Security."

William studied Shawn with interest before he extended his hand for a handshake. "Mr. Randall. Morgan, are you changing the security arrangements for the fundraiser?"

Morgan swallowed and shook her head. "No. Dad, please sit down. I must tell you something." She waited as he sat.

He studied her with a wary expression. "Okay, what is going on?"

She lowered herself into the chair next to his and reached out to touch his arm. "Yesterday someone vandalized my car and left flowers at home for me. Today I received threatening notes on the windshield."

Morgan turned and shot a warning glance at Shawn. She deliberately chose to omit any reference to the dead rabbit and the stolen clothing and hoped he wouldn't mention it.

"Dear God," William replied.

"Shawn is here as my bodyguard until this is settled."

The older man coolly appraised Shawn. "What type of experience do you have with this type of situation?"

"I'm former L.A.P.D. and then I worked for several years providing personal protection to the entertainment industry."

William turned to gaze back at her. She could see the worry in her father's eyes, and her chest tightened. "When were you going to inform me about this?"

Morgan gulped and took a deep breath. She knew this would happen and she stroked William's arm. "Dad, I don't want you to worry. I've got this under control now."

William sat back in his chair in stunned silence and then glared at Shawn. "What do you have to say about this?"

"Morgan's correct. However, her stalker has been watching her for quite a while. Only within the past twenty-four hours have things escalated."

William turned to her. "Maybe you should pull back from the fundraiser. I'll take charge if you need me to."

Morgan shook her head. This is exactly what she feared he'd say. "No, I can handle this."

Morgan shot a glance at Shawn and hoped he'd read her silent plea for support.

"Mr. Kennedy, Morgan's safe," Shawn said. "If she goes into seclusion, we risk never stopping her stalker."

William stared at Shawn and gazed at his jacket. "Are you carrying a gun?"

Shawn hesitated and cast a guilty glance at her before replying, "Yes, I am."

William's expression turned grim. "So you think this guy is dangerous?"

"Very."

"Morgan, perhaps you should move back home with your mother and I until this blows over. You shouldn't be alone at your house."

Morgan stammered, "Shawn doesn't think that would be a good idea."

"Nonsense," William snapped. "You'll be safe with us."

"I would strongly recommend against that." Shawn said.

William glared at the bodyguard, "Because?"

Morgan crossed her arms and watched the two men. Her father wasn't used to being countermanded. Shawn's polite respectful demeanor evaporated, replaced by a cool steely expression which left no doubt that he strongly disagreed with her father's suggestions.

"The threats today were directed at me. Given what's happened, I think he's quite capable of hurting anyone who stands in his way of getting to her. You, your wife, and Morgan will be at risk if she stays with you."

Morgan studied her father as he considered Shawn's point.

"What do you recommend?" William asked.

"I'm recommending she does not stay at her house alone." Shawn bit off the words 'not' and 'alone'. "My loft has restricted access. She will be far safer there than at her home at this time."

Her father frowned. "So she should move in with you?" His voice dripped with skepticism and disapproval.

"Yes, for the time being." Shawn matched her father's stare.

Morgan loosened the grip on her arms. She wasn't a psychic, and in this case she didn't need to be to have a pretty good idea of what was running through his mind. William Kennedy was a traditional man. Having his daughter move in with a man and live under the same roof wouldn't sit well with him. He was old school all the way. He glanced over at her and exhaled. "Keep me in the loop."

She nodded, surprised her father had given in so quickly. "Thanks Dad." She leaned over and gave him a hug. "I love you. This will turn out okay."

William sighed as he wrapped his arms around her. "Have you got any suggestions of how to break this to you mother? I'm all ears."

Morgan choked back a laugh. "Don't terrify her too much."

William pulled back and looked at her. "I'll try." Her father's eyes shifted to Shawn and he ordered in a firm voice, "Take care of my daughter."

"I will."

Her father then clapped his hands together. "Well, I think the web designer has done enough shopping for the time being. Let's see this auction site that's going to make a small fortune for the hospital."

She smiled at him and reached for the phone. The tension that had filled the room moments before had evaporated, and both men appeared relaxed and comfortable with each other. Within minutes they were walked through the site which had been in test mode for several days.

CHAPTER 9

The dead rabbit on the windshield had been a nice touch. When he saw the body on the side of the road, he improvised. If the man in the gray suit didn't take the warning and leave Morgan alone, let him face the consequences.

The arrival of the new guy had been a surprise. He'd been watching Morgan for weeks and there hadn't been anyone else sniffing around. The thought of the new guy being with her made him want to punch the first person who looked at him the wrong way. Morgan was meant for him, and "suit man" needed to take a hike.

She had been at the resort earlier, but he didn't need a tracking device to know that. The fundraiser auction was a few days away. Morgan would visit several times to check up on the arrangements and make any last minute adjustments. Her visits were as expected as the hundred degrees plus heat on a summer afternoon.

He quickly went to his locker and pulled out his small netbook. As he glanced around the room to confirm he was alone, he sucked a shallow, ragged breath and pressed the power button. A light glaze of sweat beaded on his brow as he sat down on the wooden bench and waited for the computer to power up.

Where was she now? He had to know. His right leg bounced on the ball of his foot as he waited. He cocked his head and listened to the muffled conversation of two men walking down the hallway. At first, he couldn't make out what they were saying, but as they approached the dressing room, their conversation became louder, easier to overhear. "Keep walking. Keep walking," he whispered.

He shoved his tongue through his lips and licked them. The two men were arguing about the Arizona Diamondbacks. "Who gives a damn about baseball?" he wondered.

The voices got fainter as the men traveled down the hall and he wiped the beads of sweat off his upper lip before he glanced down at the screen. The 'unable to connect' message flashed. "Damn."

He tightened his grip on the computer and resisted the urge to hurl it across the room. He refreshed the screen and the failed connection message appeared a second time. He shook the computer before he set it down roughly on the bench.

He glanced up. *How much time do I have left on my break?* The clock on the wall showed three forty-two. *Five minutes.* All he had left was five lousy minutes. He initiated shut down, placed the netbook in the locker, and slammed the door.

What was he going to do? She was out there, somewhere and with the "suit guy". He closed his eyes and leaned forward, resting his head on the locker door. The coolness of the metal worked like a cold compress against his forehead.

Taking a deep breath, he tried to think where Morgan would go. The store, she must be at the store. He opened his eyes and smiled. His shift would be over in six hours and then he'd go to her home. *When she comes home tonight, I'll be there.*

***

Morgan glanced over at Shawn. "Are you sure you want to do this? I mean, you don't have to."

Shawn smiled back. "I insist."

"Okay." She walked over to the safe in the work area. The nervous fluttering in her stomach returned as she turned the dial and entered the combination. He'd worked a lot of Hollywood Red Carpet events over the years and had seen many world class pieces up close. Would he like her work?

In her experience, the only time men took an interest in jewelry was when they shopped for someone. Over the years, Morgan had worked with many nervous men as they chose engagement rings. Morgan paused after he turned the handle to the safe. It wasn't long ago she had thought somewhere in the city Brad would've gone through the same ritual of selecting a ring for her. But now, she knew better. A dull heaviness settled on her and she shook it off.

Morgan scanned the trays holding the jewelry and considered what she should pull out to show Shawn. The assortment ranged from earrings to wedding rings. After a few moments of consideration, she decided to bring everything. By the time she returned to her office, Shawn had moved the items on the top of her desk back so she could spread everything out.

"Here you go." She set the velvet-clad trays on the desk and sat on the chair across from his. She studied his face, hoping she'd get a read on his thoughts. His hand reached for a bracelet and pushed it aside for a better look at a ring underneath. Morgan held her breath as her mind made the quick mental leap to his hand on her skin gently pushing back the neckline of her dress to plant a kiss.

"What do you like to design the most?"

Morgan's attention jumped back to reality. "Um," she paused to swallow and collect her words. "I don't quite know. I tend to follow my ideas as they come."

"Yet your pieces share the same design approach. They all have a sleek contemporary quality about them." He picked up a tanzanite ring. The lavender trillion was nestled in a thick wavy band of yellow gold. "I like this one. If you had added a lot of diamonds, you would've detracted from the stone."

Their eyes met, and Morgan felt drawn into him. She held her breath and drew back in her seat. His relationship with Christy made him off limits. Morgan broke eye contact and stared down at the ring. She sensed his eyes upon her as she avoided him, but she refused to meet his gaze. If she did, he might kiss her, or worse, she'd take the initiative and kiss him.

He set the tanzanite ring down and she glanced over at his hand. No wedding ring. She peeked up as Shawn turned his attention back to the jewelry. Every now and then he pulled an item out to inspect it closely.

"Morgan, you have a genuine talent for design," he said as he returned a bracelet to the tray.

She smiled. "Thanks. Coming from you it's a real compliment."

"Oh? I don't know about that. My knowledge of jewelry is pretty limited."

"I figured you've seen a lot of spectacular stuff on the Red Carpet."

"Yeah, I have. Hardly makes me an expert though." Shawn frowned as he stared blankly at the array of items before him.

Morgan froze. She had just stepped on a landmine with the reference to Los Angeles, but exactly how escaped her.

"We should leave for your house and pick up the clothes you will need for the next few days before going over to Stella's for dinner," Shawn said.

She regarded him. He appeared polite and professional. The connection she'd experienced a few moments ago had evaporated so quickly she wondered if she had imagined it.

Morgan leaned over and picked up the trays. "Yes, you're right. Let me lock this up." She walked across the room and went over to the safe. *Note to self: Keep this on a strictly business basis. Remember, when this is over, he'll be with Christy and his daughter.*

By the time she returned, Shawn had moved the items back in place on her desk. "Let me get my purse."

Within minutes, they were in his vehicle. The first thing Shawn did after starting the ignition was turn on the radio. Morgan stared out the window. She wasn't in the mood for conversation and, from the looks of things, neither was Shawn.

***

I almost kissed her. The thought pinged through Shawn's mind as he navigated out of the parking lot and headed north up Scottsdale Road. If Morgan hadn't pulled back, he would have. What was wrong with him? Clearly, he was dumb as a box of rocks and couldn't learn from past mistakes.

After all these years, he had only one simple rule. Never get emotionally involved with a client. Why was this so hard to keep? The last time he broke the rule, it nearly destroyed him.

Maybe there was a psychological term for this type of situation, like Stockholm Syndrome for hostages. Living in proximity with someone for hours every day tended to create a sense of intimacy. Perhaps that accounted for the blurred lines between common sense and desire.

Now what was he going to do? The idea of putting her up in his condo didn't appear as sound as it did earlier this afternoon but unfortunately, there weren't other options.

He pulled into the driveway at Morgan's house and turned off the ignition at the garage door.

"Give me your house keys," Shawn said.

Morgan looked at him, "My keys?"

"Yeah, I'm going in first to make sure no one's inside. Do you have the alarm on?"

"Yes, the combination is zero one zero one. The key pad is on the left side of the door."

"Okay, stay here. Lock the doors." He stepped out, and walked around the back of the house; nothing looked out of place. Shawn continued to patrol the exterior of the building and ended in the front yard. He spied Morgan sitting in the vehicle. Their eyes locked for a moment before he entered the front entrance.

Shawn took a few minutes to check the house out. After he deemed everything clear, he opened the garage door and motioned for Morgan to come inside.

"You better pack for at least a week," he said as she walked past him and through the kitchen to the other side of the house.

"Give me thirty minutes." Morgan continued down the hall to the master bedroom. Shawn took a step and stopped. Following her back there wasn't a good idea. He opened the arcadia door, and the hot humid air caused him to hold his breath as he stepped on the patio. Cumulus clouds rose up over the top of the jagged peaks of the mountains in the distance. *We're going to get another wind-storm tonight*, he thought.

He carefully made his way across the yard to the wash at the back of the property. He stepped down into the sandy trail and walked to the ironwood tree Matt had told him about earlier. When he reached the spot, he turned toward Morgan's house. His partner was correct, there was a perfect line of sight into Morgan's den through the arcadia door.

The sick son-of-a-bitch studied her like a microbe under a microscope. With the lights on and the drapes open Morgan had provided quite a show. Not intentionally of course, but the only thing better would be actual in-person contact. He shook his head and took a deep breath to release some of the tension which cinched his chest. After this ended, he'd insist she put up a solid fence, for both safety and privacy's sake.

***

Morgan removed the suitcase out of the closet and set it on the top of her bed. Pack for a week. In thirty minutes? Right, what had she'd been thinking?

First, she pulled the evening gown for the fundraiser with the shoes and coordinating purse. Next, she focused on the outfits she'd wear to work, slacks, blouses, and two dresses. She added jeans, a pair of shorts and three light weight cotton t-shirts for good measure. Then she opened her lingerie drawer and stopped.

She stared at the silky items folded in the dresser and realized she had three choices, none of which would work. A short emerald green teddy edged with black lace sat on top. Underneath laid a silk camisole with matching boxer style shorts in dusty rose and a long gown in midnight blue. "Thanks Stella, I have you to blame for this," she whispered.

At her best friend's urging, she had overhauled everything. As her relationship with Brad became exclusive, Stella masterminded a major shopping expedition to replace oversized t-shirts and flannel pajama sets into something more romantic.

"You can't let him see you in that," Stella exclaimed in mock horror when Morgan confided Brad would be spending the night. The result was a whirlwind adventure through lingerie departments of a few major department stores as well as Victoria's Secret and Fredericks of Hollywood.

Morgan had to admit the shopping spree had been fun. She didn't take long to rule out the cheesy stuff in favor of pieces that were touchable and feminine. Now she had three outfits to choose from, none of which she was comfortable wearing at Shawn's place. Morgan toyed with the idea of pulling out some sweats and a t-shirt but decided they'd be too hot to wear this time of year. She went to the closet and pulled out a terry robe which had seen better days and packed the rose camisole and boxer style shorts.

"Do you need me to take anything to the car?" Shawn asked.

Morgan whirled and found him waiting in the doorway. She wondered how long he'd been standing there watching her.

"Almost done, I need to pack my make-up but you can take the suitcase on the bed and the evening gown if you want."

He walked over, picked up the items and carried them down the hallway.

Morgan finished packing her tote bag, grabbed her purse and had proceeded halfway down the hall before Shawn came back and took the oversized canvas carryall from her.

"I've got this. Lock everything and set the alarm," he ordered.

Within minutes, they were on their way to Stella's. After Morgan gave him directions, he turned on the radio to a news station. She watched out the window. Spending the next few days under the same roof with Shawn was going to be awkward.

CHAPTER 10

"You're early. I wasn't expecting you till close to seven. Dinner won't be ready for..." Stella stopped and stared at the silent couple on her doorstep. "What happened?"

Morgan flashed a feeble smile. "It's been a long day."

"Oh, that doesn't sound good. Come in. Can I get you a drink?"

"Thanks, I'd love a glass of wine." Morgan replied quietly as she walked slowly toward the kitchen.

Stella turned to Shawn. "Is everything okay?"

"Yeah, I think I'll pass on the wine. Do you have beer?"

"Follow me." Stella said.

Something had happened and by the expressions on Morgan's and Shawn's faces it hadn't been good. By the time she'd reached the kitchen, Morgan had set out two glasses and removed a bottle of chardonnay from the refrigerator. Stella watched without comment as her friend poured a modest amount in the first glass and substantially more wine into the second one. After placing the wine back in the fridge, Morgan picked up the second glass and took a large gulp.

"Shawn, do you want a Budweiser or Coors?" Stella asked.

"I'll take a Bud, thanks."

She pulled a beer out of the fridge and turned to Shawn. "Need a glass?"

"No, I'm good." Shawn took the beer, popped the can open and took several swallows. Stella glanced sideways at Morgan. She'd set down the wineglass and stared out the kitchen window.

If I wait one of them will say something. The silence continued for several more seconds and neither appeared any closer to speaking. Stella tamped down the urge to fidget, and picked up the second glass of wine which Morgan had poured. "Okay, I give up. What went on today?"

Morgan shot a glance at Shawn.

"Go ahead. You tell her," he said.

Morgan stoked the stem of the wineglass between her thumb and forefinger. She took a deep breath and gazed up at Stella. "We were followed this morning. My stalker left a threatening letter on the SUV outside the TV station. Later at Copper Creek, he laid a dead rabbit on the windshield and another note."

"Dear God." Stella glanced over at Shawn and he nodded.

"Then you've seen him. Did you recognize him?"

"Yes, we saw him, and no, we don't know who he is," Shawn said. He then recounted a general physical description of the stalker and his car.

Stella stared back at Morgan. "Are you sure you've never seen him before?"

Morgan shook her head. "No. We didn't get a close up of his face."

"Well, how about a license number?"

"We don't have that either, right now," Shawn replied.

Stella didn't know what to say. No wonder they appeared exhausted when they arrived at her doorstep. "What did the notes say?"

"He wants Shawn to leave me alone," Morgan said.

Stella set her wineglass down and gently massaged her forehead with her fingers. "I'm sorry if I sound a little dense, but this doesn't make sense. He's stalking you, but he leaves notes for Shawn? I don't understand."

"I'm supposed to stay away from Morgan or else. I think the roadkill rabbit on the windshield is a pretty clear message of what 'or else' means." Shawn took another gulp from his beer.

Morgan added, "Shawn believes I'm not safe at my house. So, I'm moving into his place for the interim."

"For how long?" Stella asked.

"Hopefully not long; her stalker is becoming desperate. The likelihood that he'll do something reckless grows by the day. When he screws up, we'll catch him."

Stella took a deep breath and exhaled. "Or worse, hurt you both. Morgan, perhaps you shouldn't do the fundraiser. Maybe you should step back and let your father handle this."

Morgan shook her head and glanced up at her friend. Behind the worry and exhaustion, her eyes held a cool, determined glint. "Dad said the same thing this afternoon. I can't do that Stella. I'm scared he won't be able to deal with the stress and have another heart attack because of this."

"Are you sure?" Stella asked.

Morgan nodded. She glanced over at Shawn who stood calmly watching Morgan. Stella reached for her wineglass, and took another sip. She didn't know what to say. One of her friend's most admirable traits was her determination to see things through to the end. Morgan wasn't a quitter, but maybe, for once, she wasn't being wise about this.

"Stella, what's for dinner?" Shawn asked.

"Huh?" The question caught her off guard. "Oh, steak, salad, baked potatoes. Shawn, I need you to do me a favor."

"What do you need?"

"Will you barbeque the steaks? If you can't, I'll cook them on the George Forman grill." Stella smiled and batted her eyelashes playfully.

Shawn crooked a slight smile and took another swig of his beer. "I take it you don't cook outside often."

"Yep," Stella replied.

"No problem."

"Thanks. You're the man." She tipped her glass up at Shawn and smiled. Actually, she'd lied. She could easily cook on her outdoor gas barbeque, but she needed an excuse to get Shawn out of the way for a short while so she could talk with her best friend in private.

She peered over at Morgan who'd polished off about half the wine she'd poured. Stella pressed her lips together and realized she needed to get food in her friend soon. "Why don't we sit and de-compress for a bit? The potatoes are in the oven and won't be done for a while." She opened the refrigerator door, pulled out the artichoke jalapeno dip and the tortilla chips from the pantry. After setting more things on a tray, she walked to the den and set the food all down on the coffee table. She glanced behind her. Shawn had placed his hand gently on the small of Morgan's back as they came over and settled on the sofa.

They sat side-by-side. So close they almost touched each other. Shawn reclined and extended his arm along the back of the furniture behind Morgan. She reached down, lifted his beer and slid a coaster under it. He leaned forward and handed her a small cocktail napkin. Morgan scooped a chip in the dip and Shawn mirrored her actions. From Stella's perspective, it was like watching two people dance. One lead, the other followed. She stifled a grin and took a sip of her wine. "So, how did the TV interview go?"

"Okay, I think. They told us to watch the six p.m. news. Can we turn on channel eleven, please?"

Stella took the remote, turned on the television and sank back in the chair. The trio watched the newscast and, at the end of the show, the interview aired. Stella spoke after turning off the television. "Before you leave tonight we need to get on the internet and check up on the auction bids."

Shawn slowly stood up. "I'll get things started."

Once Shawn stepped outside and closed the door behind him, Stella turned to Morgan. "Okay, level with me. How are you really doing?"

"Okay considering you don't go through this stuff every day."

Morgan glanced over and checked to ensure Shawn hadn't come back inside and she took another sip of wine. "He's carrying a gun," Morgan whispered.

Stella didn't reply. What could she say to her friend? If Shawn had armed himself, then the situation had escalated to a highly dangerous state.

"I'm not completely comfortable about this," Morgan added.

"Shawn apparently thinks it necessary," Stella replied. "Remember, your stalker threatened him."

Morgan's expression shifted, and she blinked her eyes in an effort to stem the water which started to flow. She took a ragged breath. "I'm scared how this may play out. Look at me. I'm becoming a nervous wreck. I run a successful business and a major fundraiser, but now I'm being urged to go into hiding."

Stella leaned forward and softly touched Morgan's arm. "You must have faith. You've got a knowledgeable experienced person at your side. This will work itself out. You and Shawn will be fine."

Morgan stared down at the crumpled napkin in her hand and nodded. "You're right. I know you're right."

"Besides, think of the bright side. How many women can say they have a handsome man at their beck and call twenty-four hours a day? I personally could name more than a few ladies who would trade places with you in a heartbeat."

Morgan smiled and shook her head slowly. "He may be with me twenty-four hours a day, but he's not mine."

Stella swallowed back her reply. Shawn's attraction toward Morgan radiated off whenever he was within a few feet of the woman. But for some reason, Morgan either couldn't or wouldn't acknowledge this. "Can you give me a hand? I need to set the dinner table and make a salad."

"Sure, what do you want me to do?"

"Salad, I think."

Stella carried the remaining chips and dip back to the kitchen, and Morgan followed. As Morgan chopped ingredients, Stella grabbed a bottle of water and the steaks out of the refrigerator and walked out to the patio. She stepped outside and looked over at the man who closed the lid on the grill. Shawn had removed his tie but still wore his jacket and his red face reminded her of a boiled lobster. She set the platter with the meat on the side of the barbeque. "Shawn, take off your jacket. If you don't, you'll die of heat stroke and besides, Morgan saw the gun."

"She told you, huh?"

He handed her the empty beer can as he shed the clothing item and rolled up his sleeves. She took his coat and handed him the water. "Yeah, she did. She's freaked out, just in case you didn't know. Is the gun really necessary?"

"I don't want to scare either of you, but yes I think it is. This situation is becoming explosive, and Morgan has just figured it out."

"You're right. She got the message loud and clear," Stella said. "But since you've known her only a short time let me give you some insight into who Morgan Kennedy really is. After William's heart attack, everybody assumed the Kennedys would bring in outside management to run the store and fundraiser. She surprised them by stepping into her father's shoes. She's succeeded brilliantly. Her father is accustomed to calling the shots and didn't make things easy for her in the beginning, but now she's earned his trust and confidence. This business with her stalker threatens to take that away. But know this, Morgan is William Kennedy's daughter in many ways. She's a fighter."

Shawn unscrewed the cap to the water and took a large gulp before speaking. "I was in the office earlier in the day with Morgan. Her old man is a character. They are both passionate about this event being a success. How did they come up with this fundraiser?"

"She didn't tell you?"

"No." Shawn screwed the top back on the plastic container. "Shoot."

Stella grinned. "Poor word choice."

Shawn ran his hand across his forehead and wiped away sweat. "Sorry."

Stella stepped in and lowered her voice. "Morgan lost her brother, Samuel, to a swimming pool accident. He struck his head on the diving board and his death nearly tore her family apart. They started this charity fundraiser to ensure that every possible avenue of treatment is available to anyone's child in similar circumstances. This fundraiser will never be handed over for professionals to run. To the Kennedy family this is personal."

Shawn nodded as he reached over and laid the steaks on the grill. "Thanks. I figured there was a story there because she's insistent on not stepping aside. Don't be worried, I'll take good care of her."

Stella reached up and patted his arm. "I know you will."

She turned and walked back inside. Within a few minutes, Shawn joined them with the steaks. As they sat down to eat, Stella decided Morgan's stalker had been an uninvited guest at her party long enough. She took control of the conversation and spent the rest of the evening providing updates on construction projects and what her family was up to.

After dinner, they deposited the dishes into the kitchen sink and went to Stella's computer to check on the status of the online auction.

"Goodness, the weekend getaway in Sedona is up to four hundred dollars," Stella said. "Look at all the bids. With so many at this point, this is going to be a real moneymaker."

"I'll celebrate later, when everything has a bid," Morgan said.

"Your father will be extremely proud," Shawn added.

Stella glanced at Shawn. He reached over and touched Morgan's arm. Her friend's expression had changed from one of caution to a soft smile. "Thanks," she responded softly.

Stella tried not to grin as she focused back on the computer screen and scrolled down the auction listings considering what she'd bid on.

***

Where is she? He'd had been waiting for over a couple hours and Morgan still hadn't arrived at home. He left the cover of the bush and scrabbled his way out of the wash. The wind from the oncoming storm kicked up the sand which stung his eyes and buffeted him in sporadic gusts.

He crept up to the arcadia door and leaned closer, cupping the sides of his face as he peered inside. The sheer drapes were drawn, and the lights were off. He reached for the handle and pulled. No luck, it didn't budge. He stepped off the concrete patio and walked over to where that master bedroom was located. The drapes to the bedroom were drawn, but he checked the window, just in case.

Exasperated, he went to the driveway on the side of the house. He walked over and took hold of the garage door handle and jerked it. The metal door heaved slightly before settling. He checked the front driveway. No car.

She should be home now. Something is wrong. He scrambled to the front of the house and stared through the bay window. The house was silent and dark.

His heart raced. Where could she be? He threaded his fingers through his hair as he scanned the landscape and the houses in the distance. *She's with him.* The thought hit him like a hand slap. The young man dropped his hands and they tightened into fists as his fear melted into rage. He had to find her. No, find them.

He jogged back to the wash. The unevenness of the desert terrain jarred his ankles and the bushes slapped against his calves, so he slowed to a walk to avoid falling. He prepared to jump down into the sandy river bottom, then he turned and started to run back at the house. *Her home.*

"You bitch," he muttered. "You couldn't wait before you hooked up with someone new."

Morgan hurt him. Like the others. He needed to strike back. She must feel his pain and understand. The young man reached down and picked up a medium sized river rock and with a gut-wrenching scream he hurled it. The stone fell short of the large glass door landing with a heavy thud on the concrete patio before rolling haphazardly to a stop several feet short of his target. He grabbed another one and charged up to the patio. With all his strength he launched the rock at the arcadia door. At first he thought the glass held. The crash and tingle of falling debris actually sounded like what he heard on the television shows. The drapes swayed back and then returned, covering the rock's disappearance into the dark interior.

Within seconds, the security alarm sounded. The high pitch wail reminded him of an upset woman crying in protest. He grinned and ran. The police would arrive soon, followed by Morgan. Forget chasing her down. This time she'd come to him.

CHAPTER 11

Morgan stared at Stella's computer screen. If the brisk bidding continued, this year's fundraiser might raise the largest amount in the event's twelve year history. She leaned back in the chair, inhaled slowly and tamped down the impulse to jump up and do the happy dance. Instead, she pressed the fingers to her lips to hide her grin as Stella scanned the list of items up for bid.

After they finished, the trio returned to the den, and Morgan's cell phone rang. She retrieved it out of her purse and checked caller ID. She shot a glance at Shawn who was sliding on his jacket. "It's the security company who monitors my house."

His eyes took a suspicious expression. "Answer it."

She put the phone up to her ear. "Hello?"

"Ms. Kennedy, this is Home Security Solutions. Your alarm has been tripped. Are you safe?"

"Yes, but I'm not at home."

"The police have been notified and are on their way. Can you meet them there?"

"Hold please. Shawn, my house has been broken into. The police are coming, we need to go back."

He shifted his holster and pistol into place under his jacket. "I'm not sure that's such a good idea. I suspect your stalker is trying to get you to surface."

"But the police will be there. We can give them information and they will canvas the area. They might catch him." Morgan said.

Shawn didn't appear convinced. Finally he replied, "All right, but I don't want you to leave my side. If I think things are unsafe and tell you to get in the car or we're leaving, we do it. No discussion. This isn't negotiable."

She nodded and turned to Stella. "Thanks for dinner."

"Anytime, please keep me in the loop," Stella said.

Morgan gave her friend a hug. "Absolutely."

She counted three patrol cars stationed in the driveway and in front of her house when they arrived. A policeman standing guard regarded them cautiously as they stepped out of the SUV.

"Are you the homeowner?" The officer asked.

"Yes." Morgan replied.

"Someone threw a rock through your arcadia door. The alarm has been turned off, and the house is clear."

Shawn interjected. "Did any of the patrol cars report seeing an older Honda Accord in the area?"

The officer appraised Shawn with a no-nonsense expression which Morgan found intimidating, but Shawn appeared unfazed. He stared back at the policeman with a quiet focus which left no doubt he expected an answer.

"Why do you ask?" the cop asked.

"Ms. Kennedy has a stalker. We believe he drives a car of that make and model," Shawn said.

The officer shifted his gaze from Shawn to Morgan. She tensed and braced herself for the upcoming questions. Instead, Shawn softly placed his hand on the small of her back. The simple gesture spoke volumes to her. *You're not alone.*

"Go around to the back and talk to Officer Williams," the policeman instructed.

"Thank you." Shawn reached over and gently placed his hand on her arm before they walked back to the driveway and to the patio. As they turned the corner, Morgan saw one officer standing near the arcadia door and two in the yard patrolling with flashlights. The metal door frame was open with the drapes pulled back, and shards of glass shimmered like an array of diamonds on the tile floor.

She and Shawn walked up to the policeman standing at the door. "Officer Williams?" Morgan asked.

The officer gave both of them a quick visual once over before speaking. "Are you the owner?"

"Yes, what happened?" Morgan replied.

"Someone tried getting in and broke your door. We've already gone inside. It's empty, but you should check to see if anything is missing."

Morgan swallowed, and her mouth went dry.

"Officer, did anyone observe an older model burgundy Honda Accord in the area?" Shawn asked.

The policeman shook his head. "No. We think he came up from the wash and had left long before we got here."

Shawn nodded and began to give the officer a recap of her circumstances. Morgan walked past the two men and stepped inside. Glass shards crunched beneath the balls of her shoes as she tiptoed across the tile floor. Someone had turned on the lights, which was a good thing as it reduced the "someone has been in my house" factor a notch.

She scanned the room, and found nothing else had been disturbed. In the background, she heard Shawn's voice and she waited, frozen, unable to go further in the home. Despite the July heat, a numbing chill wrapped itself around her.

Shawn walked up behind her and gently laid his hand on her shoulder. "Do you want to walk your house?"

She turned and looked at him. Part of her wanted to check things out and confirm nothing had been taken, and the other part of her yearned to run and hide. "I guess so."

Morgan walked through the kitchen and down the hall with Shawn close behind. His quiet presence gave her courage. This was her house but thanks to this idiot, right now she didn't feel safe here.

As they entered the master bedroom, Morgan's eyes traveled to the dresser, half expecting to find the drawer open and more lingerie missing. But it was closed. She walked over to the closet, her stomach tensed and she took a deep breath as she prepared to open the door. A quick mental collage of images from a horror film threaded through her mind. *The closet, he's in the closet. The bad guy always hides in the closet.* She opened the door firmly and realized no one was inside, and all her clothes were untouched. She exhaled and the muscles in her shoulders loosened a notch.

She and Shawn moved on to check the guest bedroom and then the office. Each time, the same routine, exploring closets, drawers and even once under the bed hunting for her personal bogeyman. When they finished, they returned to the arcadia door.

"Any luck on the patrols?" Shawn asked.

"Nothing, looks like your guy is long gone," Williams replied. "You may want to see if you can get this boarded up for tonight."

"No, I've got a contact for emergency glass installation." Morgan replied, as she pulled out her phone. Within a few minutes, she had contacted the company the jewelry store used and arranged a repair man to come out for a door replacement.

The officers came in from canvassing the yard and gradually departed, leaving Morgan and Shawn alone.

***

He jumped into the sandy wash and sprinted to his car. As soon as the engine started, he changed gears and sped away. As he traveled west, the police cars appeared. One came from Tatum Road and the other from a side street. Both vehicles had their emergency lights flashing, but their sirens weren't on.

Did they think they would catch him by getting there silently? He grinned as they faded from sight in his rear view mirror. Now all he had to do is stay away for a little while. Give them time to investigate and for Morgan to arrive.

Morgan would come to secure her house. This time, when she left, he'd follow her. This should teach her a lesson. She'd never get away from him. He pulled into a Jack-in-the-Box restaurant and parked the car. He laid his head against the seat's head rest and conjured Morgan in his mind. Her golden brown eyes emerged from the darkness. She looked concerned, sorry for what she'd done. "Good," he murmured.

He glanced down at his wristwatch, noted the time, before he unbuckled his seatbelt and shifted to reach back to his pocket to retrieve his wallet. After counting his money, he decided to order a large Coke. This promised to be a long night and he could use the caffeine.

***

Shawn opened the front door to his loft. Morgan waited in the hallway as he stepped in and turned on the lights. As she entered, Morgan found out what Scottsdale loft living was like. The open floor plan highlighted the dark wood floors, leather furniture and drop dead gorgeous view of the urban skyline. She gazed through the glass door which lead to his patio and faced south into downtown Scottsdale. The city lights twinkled and gave the room a soft glow. Morgan knew she should say something but somehow, "wow" didn't seem to be quite enough.

He walked around her and said, "I'm putting you up in this bedroom."

With her suitcase in one hand and the evening gown hanging in a garment bag in the other, he led her past the dining area and down a short hall.

"Bathroom is here, and you make a sharp turn to your bedroom." He walked in, flipped on the light switch, dropped the suitcase on the bed, and walked to the closet and hung her dress.

She took a deep breath. A large double bed with a brass headboard was draped in a lavender floral comforter and solid colored pillow shams. Pictures of Winnie the Pooh characters had been framed and arranged in a gallery on the wall. This room belonged to his daughter.

She gazed over at Shawn "What's her name?"

He regarded her. His eyes held a wary expression and his lips were pressed together firmly. Morgan smiled in an effort to encourage an answer. "What's your daughter's name?"

"Emma," he replied. "Her name is Emma."

"That's a lovely name. How old is she?" Morgan guessed by the decor the girl couldn't be more than seven or eight.

"She's six."

"I didn't know that you're married. Will I meet your wife and daughter?"

"I'm not married," he answered abruptly as he walked toward the door. "Let me know if you need anything."

Morgan watched him retreat. Not married? Strange he didn't speak of a divorce. In her experience, divorced men eagerly talked about - no, complained- about their ex-wives. He was so reluctant to tell her his daughter's name. Why?

She glanced around and thought about the living room with its view. This loft must've cost him some serious money and appeared to be an odd choice to raise a child in. However, if Emma is Christy Thomas's daughter, having a quiet, secure, paparazzi-free location would be an absolute necessity.

She turned and started unpacking her suitcase. The drawers on the dresser held Emma's clothes, so she settled on taking the extra hangers in the closet and hanging as much of her clothing as she could. Finally, she lifted the suitcase off the bed and deposited it on the floor of the walk-in closet. She'd fish her way through the rest of her clothes as she needed them. She picked up the tote bag with her makeup and headed to the bathroom. As she stacked the toiletries on the counter, she heard a shower on the other side of the condo.

Morgan finished, returned to the bedroom, stripped out of her dress and threw on her robe. A hot shower should help her relax enough to get a good night's sleep.

After the shower, she slid into the teddy and shorts. The steam from the shower caused the soft fabric to cling to her damp skin. She opened the door to the bathroom slightly and peered out. The loft was quiet, and the lights were out. She scurried down the hall.

Once inside the bedroom, she flung the robe on the dresser and proceeded to pull the comforter back. Suddenly she froze. She wasn't alone, and as she turned she caught Shawn standing at the doorway. She winced as she realized with the stickiness of the silk on her skin he must've gotten quite a view of her. She scrambled over, grabbed her robe and slid into it. Once she had tied the sash, she looked up and crossed her arms across her chest.

"Is there something you need?" Despite her attempt to appear nonchalant, her voice sounded breathy and nervous.

He broke his gaze and glanced down at the floor. Shawn wore a pair of faded five-o-one jeans and his damp hair was finger-combed away from his face.

"Sorry, I didn't mean to intrude. I wanted to find out what the schedule is for tomorrow."

She slowly dropped her arms as she realized he was uncomfortable too. "I planned to spend most of the day at the store, but I need to go back to Copper Creek in the afternoon. Also, I forgot to tell you this, but I'll be spending the night after the fundraiser at the resort. Things will end late, so it'll be easier to take a room."

Shawn nodded. "Do you have your room booked?"

"I've booked a suite. My parents are supposed to have the room on the other side. Do you want it?"

He paused and a tiny upturn to his lips appeared as if he was amused by a private joke.

"Would your parents mind if they got bumped?"

"Probably not, I'll make arrangements tomorrow."

"Thanks. Goodnight." He turned and closed the door behind him as he left.

Morgan exhaled and ran her hand through her hair. What was that all about? Earlier he practically bolted out of the room and appeared to be avoiding her, now he shows up without warning. She waited a couple minutes and listened. Once she was sure he wasn't returning she shed her robe and crawled in bed.

He walked into the store and Morgan looked up from the display case at him but she couldn't make out his face.

"Morgan, I've come for you" It was him! The faceless man extended his hand for her.

She turned and darted out the back door before he cleared the display cases. She slammed through the fire door in the storage area and raced down the alley. She didn't know where to run to, all she knew was to run away from him. He followed her. She could sense him catching up. Afraid to look over her shoulder and slow down, she sprinted on. The pounding of his feet on the asphalt behind her grew louder.

She pushed harder. Her heart pounded, and her lungs burned as she tried to continue her flat out run. Scrambling into the un-developed desert at the edge of the shopping center, she darted through the scrub and cactus. Her clothing caught and was tugged and yanked by the vegetation. The wind kicked up, and angry storm clouds darkened the sky with flashes of lightning and the low growl of thunder. Morgan cast a glance over her shoulder as he closed in and grabbed her.

"No, get away from me." Morgan screamed as she flailed her arms violently to toss him off.

Morgan awoke with a jolt. The beat of her heart thudded in her ears, and she drew quick short breaths. Suddenly a flicker of light appeared outside the bedroom window, and within moments the rumble of thunder followed. She lay down on the sheet, pulled the comforter up, and stared up at the ceiling. Another lightning flash exploded, and the crash of thunder sounded before the light faded. The window rattled violently, and she squeezed her eyes shut in an effort to block out the storm.

After several minutes of listening to the creak of the windows and the boom of thunder, Morgan slid out of bed, put on her robe, and walked into the living room. The drapes to the sliding door on the balcony weren't drawn, and she watched the storm tear across the night sky.

"Morgan, are you all right?"

She jumped and then shoved her hands into the terrycloth pockets in an effort to look relaxed. "I'm fine." But she wasn't, the lie was obvious.

Shawn moved closer and stood next to her.

She turned away and stared at the glass door. "I'm okay. I had a nightmare." She peered over at him. A flicker of lightning lit up his face. His blue eyes focused on her. Her first thought was that he'd think she was a drama queen, but the worry mirrored back at her from his eyes made her chest tighten.

"I'm sorry I woke you up. Go back to bed. I'll be..." She stopped, unable to finish the sentence as her lips trembled. She took a deep breath and pressed her lips tightly together. *He must think I'm an idiot.* Morgan closed her eyes in an effort to stop them from watering further. She wouldn't cry.

Shawn stepped over to the end table and turned on the lamp.

She crossed her arms and stared back at him hoping to bluff her way through this with a show of strength. "I dreamt of my stalker. He chased and caught me." Shawn moved closer and wrapped his arms around her, drawing her to him.

"Breathe."

Morgan melted into him as she wrapped her arms around his waist. She felt the steady rise and fall of his chest. He reached down and pushed a tendril of hair off her face as she gazed up at him.

Shawn's eyes darkened, and he slid his hand under her chin and gently lifted it. He lowered his lips closer. She closed her eyes and waited, but he didn't kiss her. He was so close. She could feel his warm breath caressing her cheeks.

Please, she silently prayed.

His lips softly touched hers. Morgan slid her arms around his neck. The kiss deepened, and she felt his tongue tease her lips. He pulled back and slowly his lips traveled across her cheek and down her throat. Morgan sucked in a breath and held it as she tilted her head, giving him greater access. He nuzzled her and returned to her lips. This time the kiss was followed by an almost imperceptible nibble on her lower lip. She pulled back and opened her eyes. Shawn's lips curled into a soft smile, and he leaned in again for another kiss.

Morgan slid her hand from his neck and down his chest where she paused. She swore she could feel the steady thud of his heart. Her fingers traveled lower and he tensed, released her, and pulled back out of her arms.

What had happened?

"I'm sorry," Shawn said. His voice was low, guttural and breathless.

Morgan paused. Did she hear him correctly? She studied his face. His expression was a mixture of anticipation and regret. Her lips tingled, and she took a step back. *He was turning her down?* She threaded her hand through her hair and swept it back from her face. "What?" She whispered.

"I can't do this Morgan. I'm sorry, I've stepped over a line I shouldn't have."

His flushed face and rapid breath meant he was interested. Morgan resisted looking lower, but she'd bet he was more than interested. "I don't understand…"

"Look, let's chalk this one up to us getting caught up in the moment."

Morgan felt as if she'd been slapped. *Oh my God. He still loves her.*

She shoved her hands into the robe's pockets. "I'm sorry. I misunderstood. You said you weren't married, and I assumed you were divorced. Had I known you two were still together…" Morgan stopped, fearing to finish the sentence out loud.

"I'm not divorced."

She glanced up and took a deep breath. "Okay, you're going to have to help me here. I'm a little confused. What exactly is your status?"

He dropped his gaze, and his eyes traveled the room. He looked everywhere but at her.

"Christy and I were never married. When the job ended, we went our separate ways."

"But you have a daughter," Morgan said.

Shawn gave a short cynical laugh. "Yeah, we do. I didn't know about the pregnancy until weeks later. I offered to marry her, but getting married to her bodyguard would've ended everything she worked for."

He stopped talking and stared out the window. The grief and regret in his voice was impossible to miss. Morgan tamped down the urge to walk over and touch him.

"I fought for custody of my daughter, and we came to an out-of-court arrangement. I'm not supposed to talk about what happened. No interviews, no tell-all books, absolutely no publicity. In exchange, I got a chance to start over and be with Emma several times per year."

Morgan listened in silence. Now the pieces fit. The fleeting moments of warmth and the retreat to professional detachment that always followed. He'd been hurt, and in no way would he sign up for that kind of pain again.

"I don't know what to say. I'm sorry."

Shawn shot a look at her. "Promise you won't say anything about Christy and Emma. You can't go public, or there will be hell to pay."

His eyes held a mix of concern and firmness which led her to believe that if she didn't agree she'd see a side of him she'd rather not know existed. "Okay?" he pressed.

"Absolutely, I won't say a word."

He flashed a relieved smile. "Good."

Morgan crooked a smile. "Good? That's all it took? Whew! That was easy. What happens if I do a National Enquirer interview? Do you have to kill me?"

Shawn smirked back. "That might be a problem. I'm supposed to protect you."

Morgan broke eye contact and stared at the skyline outside the window. Her stalker, this unknown man, haunted her like a ghost.

"See you tomorrow," Shawn said.

Morgan continued to stare out the window. "Good night."

Shawn waited a few seconds as if he wasn't certain what to do next. Then without another word, he turned and walked to his bedroom. As the distance between them grew, a chill settled on her shoulders and seeped into her. The door to his bedroom closed with a soft thump and a click as the latch caught.

She brought her fingers to her lips. What would happen when her stalker was caught? The thought that she and Shawn would go their separate ways made her heart ache. *Dear God, what have I gotten myself into now?*

CHAPTER 12

The lightning fingered across the night sky and growls of thunder always followed. Even here, in the parking lot, his car rocked gently as gusts of wind buffeted it. He glanced at his wristwatch. Two hours had passed since he broke Morgan's arcadia door. The police should've left and he guessed it would be safe to drive back to her house. Right now, Morgan would be fighting a losing battle to keep wind and sand out of her house. "Serves her right," he muttered. Morgan would have to learn if she didn't do what he wanted, she'd pay the price.

He started the engine and eased his car out of the parking lot. His fingers tapped nervously on the steering wheel. More than anything, he'd like to push his vehicle a little faster, but the last thing he needed right now was to get pulled over for speeding. The police were on patrol, and tripping up on the little stuff could bring his plans to a screeching halt.

Twenty minutes later, he turned down the single lane road which led to the development where Morgan's home sat. The street appeared quiet and there was not a patrol car in sight. *So far so good.* Her house appeared in the beams of his car's headlights and he turned his lights off and did a slow drive-by.

The house was dark. He scanned the front yard and peered at the windows in an effort to find some sign of life inside. Where was she? The question ricocheted in his mind like a stray bullet. "She has to be here," he whispered.

He doubled back for a second look. "What the hell?" he hissed.

Pressing the accelerator, he sped up, made a right turn and headed for the dip in the road which crossed the wash. He'd have to check this out on foot, but he must hurry. Leaving the car by the road would attract the attention of anyone who drove by. Still, he had to know if Morgan was there.

He pulled the car off to the side and turned the engine off. He swung the door open and stepped into the sandy soil. The hair on his arms tingled just before the sky crackled and hissed above him, and a lightning bolt lit up the darkness. For a few seconds, the desert looked as if someone had turned on a light switch. A boom of thunder erupted before the light completely faded. The concussion rolled through his chest like a bomb, and he instinctively flinched from the noise.

As the thunder softened, he straightened and considered what to do next. -His sensible side told to return to the relative safety of the car and leave, but the other side, the inner voice that knew his dreams, screamed at him to continue down the sandy dry creek.

First a small step, a hesitation, and then another one. *God, I have to know.* He began to scramble down the wash to her home.

The brush thinned out, and the young man dropped to his knees and crawled the last thirty yards commando style. As he reached the ironwood tree and shrubbery, he stood up and peered across the lot to the back of her house.

He stared at the patio, blinked, and looked again. "What the...." The glass arcadia door was intact. For a few seconds, he wondered if he'd imagined hurling the river rock earlier this evening.

"No!" The man swung his arm and slapped the bushes in frustration. He'd been so sure that this would work, but Morgan had given him the slip again. What was he going to do now? He toyed with crawling out of the wash and breaking the door again. No, too risky. He turned and began the hike back to his car. Tomorrow, he'd go to the store.

***

I must get some sleep. But after what happened earlier, she couldn't. Christy left Shawn. What happened? Granted, Morgan would be the first to admit she didn't know everything about him, but she understood one thing. Shawn loved his daughter and wouldn't run away from his responsibilities. The picture of the three of them on Shawn's office wall floated in her mind like a ghost. They looked so happy together. Morgan sat up in the bed, then fluffed and stacked the pillows before laying back on them. "This is ridiculous. You've known this man less than twenty-four hours, and you're worried about his former love live. Come on, get a grip."

She reached for the remote control on the nightstand and turned on the small TV on the dresser. After turning the volume down, she scrolled through the channels before settling on HGTV.

The last thing she remembered was watching a bulldozer remove old shrubs for a front yard remodel.

Morgan awoke to sunlight filtering through the blinds and glanced over at the bedroom clock, seven thirty. She turned off the TV and listened. The condo was silent, so Shawn must not be up yet. Slipping out of bed she picked up a change of clothes, her robe and headed for the bathroom. Flipping on the light, she glanced in the mirror. Her eyes were still a bit puffy from last night. Getting ready to face the world would require some extra effort this morning.

When she emerged, the smell of fresh brewed coffee wafted through the air. After dropping off her clothes in the bedroom, Morgan walked to the kitchen. She paused briefly at the end of the hallway and spied Shawn standing behind the counter with the newspaper spread out in front of him.

His hand rested on the granite countertop, and a coffee mug lay within easy reach. A nervous flutter rippled through her. Morgan felt like she was in some weird version of the morning after even though technically they hadn't done anything. *What's he going to say this morning?* She swallowed and took a breath as she studied him.

Shawn turned the page on the paper. His hair was tousled, and the dark growth on his jaw line indicated he hadn't shaved. A navy polo shirt skimmed his chest and fell below the waistband on the faded jeans. She couldn't tell from this vantage point, but she'd bet he was barefoot. He owned a just-rolled-out-of-bed air about him that she found delicious.

"Good morning," she said softly.

He glanced up at her and smiled. "How do you take your coffee?"

"Sugar and cream."

He turned and pulled another mug out of the cabinet and proceeded to pour her a cup. Morgan slid onto the bar stool across the counter from him. She peeked down. *Sports pages.*

"They've printed an article on the fundraiser." He handed her the mug, reached over and picked up the newspaper on his right. She noted he hadn't only pulled the section out for review but had folded the paper in such a way that the article was the first thing for her to read.

"Thanks." Morgan took the paper. She read while she sipped the coffee. The reporter had done an excellent job of promoting where the funds went for this event. The family was mentioned as longtime supporters. She felt a soft pang of disappointment as she noted her brother Samuel wasn't mentioned. After all these years, time had erased how his death had played a critical role in starting this fundraiser. She set the paper down. Shawn still reviewed the sports section.

What is it about guys and sports? She wondered. Her father and Brad did the same thing. They read that section of the newspaper first and would discuss, for what seemed like hours, the status of injuries and trades of the local teams.

"What do you want for breakfast?"

She glanced up from the newspaper. "I usually don't do breakfast."

Shawn grinned. "You're kidding. Breakfast is the most important meal of the day."

She smiled back. "So I've been told, toast?"

"Come on, you need some protein. How do you like your eggs?"

"Doesn't matter, scrambled, I guess."

He pulled out a carton from the fridge and a skillet from the side drawer at the bottom of the stove. As he turned away, Morgan took the opportunity to check him out. *Nice.* She glanced back to the paper as he stood up. Memories of last night, when he walked into the bedroom and caught her in the teddy flashed through her mind. She took another sip of coffee and tamped down her embarrassment. "I'm a little surprised at you fixing breakfast. You didn't strike me as the domestic type."

He pulled a spatula out and turned on the burner. "Yeah, that's me. I'm full of surprises."

Morgan smiled. "Do you cook a lot?"

"When I get a chance," Shawn said.

"Okay, everybody's got a specialty. What's your signature dish?"

"Let me think."

Morgan watched him as he pulled out a glass bowl, picked up an egg and cracked it, singlehandedly. After adding a second and a third one, he took a fork and whisked them.

Impressive, she thought. Who knew when she hired a bodyguard she would get an Iron Chef in the deal too.

"Pancakes."

"Huh?" Morgan snapped back to attention.

"I would say pancakes. Emma loves my pancakes."

Morgan laughed. "Now you tell me."

He grinned as he dropped the bread in the toaster and pushed down the handle. "I'll make pancakes tomorrow if we have time."

He'd brought up Emma and he appeared relaxed talking about her. Morgan took another sip of coffee before posing her next question. "How does she like them, Maple syrup and butter?"

"She likes a hearty breakfast. She spreads peanut butter on them before adding the syrup."

"Really, I've never heard of anyone doing that."

"My daughter adds peanut butter to about anything she can. I should have taken stock out in Peter Pan or Jiff years ago."

Morgan grinned. "Actually, it does sound kinda good. How often does she visit?"

"I get her for four weeks in the summer, and we alternate the major holidays. Sometimes when Christy is on a location that isn't conducive to having a child on set, I'll take her."

"Has she already been here or is she coming?"

"She'll be here in a couple of weeks."

Morgan nodded and wondered if her stalker situation would be over by then. If not, she supposed her case would get handed over to someone else. She took another sip of coffee and decided to not bring up the question.

"When do we need to be over at the resort?" Shawn asked as he drizzled a small amount of olive oil into the frying pan.

"You use olive oil and not butter?"

"Heart healthy fat."

"Oh." Morgan said. "We need to check in late this afternoon with Ellen. Other than that things are pretty quiet. Today is the calm-before-the-storm day."

Shawn moved the eggs around the skillet, silent for a few moments before he spoke. "I'll need to run to my office for a short while. You have a choice. You can either come with me or stay at the store. If you stay at the store, you must not be on the sales floor. I want you behind the locked security door, and you can't pick up any phone calls directly. Let them go to voice mail."

Morgan set the coffee cup down and stared into the dark brew. Did Shawn's trip to the office have to do with her case? Since he didn't volunteer any information she checked her thoughts. *I'm getting paranoid.* Besides, the downtime at the store would give her a chance catch up on paperwork. "I need to get some work done at the store," she said.

He looked up from the skillet and threw her a serious glance. "You must do exactly what I say about staying out of sight. Your stalker will be anxious to find you today. The store is one of the first places he'll look."

Morgan watched as he ladled the eggs and placed a slice of toast on a plate before handing it to her. "No problem."

***

"Matt asked to speak with you as soon as you got in."

Shawn nodded acknowledgement to the receptionist and walked in the front entrance. When he reached the door, he spied his partner hunched over a series of printouts. "What's up?"

Matt glanced up from his paperwork. "They got a couple prints off Morgan's car and a partial off the water bottle. They belong to the same guy."

Shawn sat down the chair opposite Matt's desk. "Now we're sure he's been watching her at home too."

"Yeah, the police are still running them through the system. We're out of luck if the guy has no criminal history."

"Last night he threw a rock and broke Morgan's arcadia door. We had to meet with the police and get the door replaced."

Matt shook his head and cracked a wry grin. "Whew! Things keep getting better and better," Matt said. "How much longer do you think this will continue?"

Shawn shrugged. "Hard to say. He's smart, persistent and pissing the hell out of me, but so far he hasn't done anything stupid enough to get caught."

Matt sat back in his chair. "How's Morgan holding up?"

"As well as can be expected, she had a nightmare last night that woke both of us up," Shawn said.

Matt cocked an eyebrow and waited for Shawn to elaborate. "And?"

He glared back at his partner. Shawn didn't like the inference that something between them had happened, and he damned sure wasn't going to mention what could've happened. "She's taking a room at the resort tomorrow afternoon and spending the night after the auction. It's a suite, and I don't want to be in the adjoining room, but we will need coverage. I would like to have Sabrina in the other bedroom. I'll take a separate room nearby."

Matt played with a pen in his hands as he listened. "Any problems?"

"No, and I don't want any to start."

"Do you need Sabrina on duty for the whole day or as Morgan's roommate for tomorrow night?"

"I need her present from early afternoon on."

Matt exhaled. "Okay, I'll set things up and have Laura get you a room reservation as well."

"Thanks." Shawn stood up and walked out of the office. When he reached the door, he paused, resisting the impulse to turn around and look at Matt. If he did, Shawn knew he wouldn't like what he would see.

***

He stood at the sink shoveling spoonful after spoonful of sugary cereal into his mouth, sweet and crunchy, the perfect combination. Most people gave up eating children's cereal by his age, but he had to thank his grandmother. She knew it was his favorite and always kept the pantry well-stocked.

Today he'd spend his time hanging out around the store. Morgan had to show eventually and this was his best shot of finding her. But he had one problem; his car. They knew the make and model he drove because the man had noticed him yesterday when he'd followed them in the SUV.

He toyed with renting something to drive, but the cost pushed that option out of reach. So he'd borrow his grandmother's car as much as he loathed the idea. If his old run down car was a POS, then hers was a major league POS. Old, big, boxy, and a complete gas hog to boot. Yet, he knew he could borrow it and she'd ask few questions as to why.

His grandmother stiffly ambled into the kitchen. She always moved slowly in the morning. She walked over, picked up the carton of milk off the counter, and placed it in the refrigerator. He studied her hands. Long ago, they must've been delicate and beautiful, but now arthritis had transformed them into something more deformed than normal.

His grandmother, more than anyone else in life he knew, deserved a break in life. No matter what happened, she always stood by him. Unlike his mother, who kicked him to the curb over a one-night-stand several years ago. He stared out the kitchen window. The memory flooded back and he tightened his fingers on the bowl.

He opened his bedroom door to the sound of a crash and the stinging smack of skin on skin. "Mom?

His mother stood with her hand on the side of her face, and a mountain of a man faced her, weaving on his legs. The stranger glanced down the hall and hissed "Oh hell."

His mothered spoke, "Frank, go back to bed"

The eleven year old boy couldn't move. The man growled. "You heard her. If you know what's good for you, you'll return to your bedroom."

His mother's eyes pleaded with him. "It's okay, honey. Go to bed."

The man snatched her arm and jerked her around. Then it happened. Something inside the boy snapped. All this thug cared about was making sure her son wasn't under foot. "You heard your mother," he shouted.

Frank clenched his fists and bit his lower lip. "No."

The man stopped as if the boy's answer surprised him. Then he released his mother's arm. "I'm leaving. I don't need this."

"No, stay." The woman pleaded as she reached for his arm. "Let me talk to him."

The man snorted and gestured to the boy. "Fine, you handle it."

His mother dropped her hand from his arm and took a few hesitant steps toward her son. The skin on her cheek was pink and a tear traced down her cheek. She took a ragged deep breath before speaking. "Frank, everything is fine. Go to bed. I'll talk with you in the morning."

The boy stared at her and then at the man who sniped. "Doesn't mind you very well, does he?"

To this day Frankie can't recall the exact details of what happened next. But a tidal wave of anger and frustration breached the walls of his contained frightened existence. He wasn't scared anymore.

He charged with a blood-curdling scream that caused the man to stagger back a few steps from the force of his cry. His mother shrieked as she tried to grab him as he flew past her but Frank twisted, shoved, and jerked from her grasp.

"Jesus," the man said. He stepped back where his calves caught on the glass coffee table. At eleven, the boy was barely ninety-five pounds and was not a match for the man in a straight up battle, but booze and amazement tipped the scales against the drunk. The boy stiffened his arms and slammed into the man's paunchy gut. The man's eyes widened in surprise and his arm flailed in the air as he tumbled down onto the coffee table behind him. The sound of shattering glass traveled through the air, then a scream from the man.

"Oh God," the man whined as he reached down and grasped his thigh and writhed in pain. Frank looked down. The red spots of blood grew larger, soaking his jeans.

"What have you done?" his mother cried.

"Help me," the man pleaded.

His mother wheeled around and grabbed her son's arm. "Look at what you've done."

He gazed at his mother's face. The mascara had streaked from the tears and the remains of the bright lipstick she'd worn earlier that evening made her look like a battered tragic version of a clown.

She ran to the kitchen and returned with towels and began to apply pressure to the man's leg. She glared at her son. "Get out of here she ordered.

Frankie stepped back. He'd won and what did he get for defending her? She got angry with him. Not the drunkard she brought home and who roughed her up, but her own son.

The man latched eyes with him and growled. "When I get back from the hospital you better not be here."

Frank flipped him the finger and spun around and dashed back to his room. After they left for the emergency room, he called his grandmother. He moved out before they returned and he'd never gone back. His mother made her bed. Let her sleep in it, with whoever would have her.

"Are you still hungry? Do you want me to make you some eggs or toast?" The young man snapped out of his thoughts and glanced at his grandmother. Her gray hair was pulled into a bun and she wore a simple house dress which had seen better days. He briefly wondered how long she had owned it.

"No, I'm fine. But I need a favor."

"What?" she asked quietly.

"Can I borrow your car?" He paused, then continued. "Mine's running hot. I think I need to have the radiator flushed and I'm afraid if I drive my car it will overheat on the way to work."

Concern graced her brown eyes, and he could almost read her thoughts regarding the prospect of another car bill. "Sure. Are you sure it's just the radiator? I can help with the bill if you need."

"No, I'm sure a radiator flush will solve the problem. Thanks."

His chest tightened in response to her worried expression. He stepped forward and kissed her on the cheek. The old woman wrapped her arms around him and gently squeezed a hug back in return. He stiffened and pulled back. "I've got to get ready for work."

He turned and forced himself not to bolt from her. He had places to go and one very special person to catch up with.

CHAPTER 13

Morgan stared at the computer screen and didn't believe what she saw. Every auction item had a bid. She whipped out a calculator and added up the total revenue. She sat back, rolled the leather chair away from the desk and did a sitting happy dance. "Yes, yes, yes!"

Wait till her father heard about this. He'd been so concerned an online auction wouldn't work, but she'd been right. She picked up the phone and dialed her parent's home number.

"Hello?"

"Mom, can I speak to Dad?"

Her mother's voice turned serious. "What's wrong?"

"Nothing, for the first time in a couple of days absolutely nothing," Morgan replied. "I'm on the auction site and every item has a bid. Can you believe it?"

"Oh honey, that's great," her mother replied. "Your father should be here anytime now. I'll tell him."

"Thanks, Mom, don't say anything about this. Let me surprise him."

"Fine, how are *you* doing?"

Her mother's question caused Morgan's smile to fade, and she took a deep breath and exhaled. "I'm okay. Right now, I'm locked away in the back of the store. Shawn had to make a trip to his office and should be back shortly."

"You're all by yourself?"

"Mom, don't worry. I'm fine. No one, outside of the staff, knows I'm in here."

Elaine Kennedy didn't comment for a few moments. "I hope you're correct."

Morgan pressed her lips together and bit back a reply. Her mother's worry and skepticism was understandable, but her concern about being alone at the store made Morgan edgy. Over the years, her mom had demonstrated time and again an uncanny way of anticipating things before they happened. More than women's intuition, both Morgan and her sister Victoria were half convinced her mother possessed some level of psychic ability.

"Do you have a feeling?" Morgan asked.

"Nothing specific," the older woman replied.

Morgan raked her fingers through her hair and sank back in her chair. Her mother's feelings or hunches were hard to deal with. She in effect delivered a "you've been warned" notice without exactly giving you anything specific you could actually do something about.

"Mom, I need a favor."

"What?"

"Shawn would like to have your room at Copper Creek tomorrow night. I'll get you another room for the night. Okay?"

Her mother laughed. "Fine, I'm looking forward to meeting your *bodyguard* tomorrow."

"Mom, he's just doing his job."

"Of course," her mother's voice sounded suitably serious, but Morgan sensed that the woman was grinning on the other end of the phone.

"Thanks. I'll set up a reservation for your room right now. Have dad give me a call when he gets in."

"I will and Morgan, please be careful."

Morgan hung up the phone, sank back in the chair and mulled the conversation over. No matter what good happened, her stalker cast a shadow on her life. This needed to end and soon.

***

Frank surveyed the parking lot searching for an open parking space. The old battleship of a car needed room and he'd been reduced to strategizing where to beach it. Spying a few open spaces at the back of the shopping center, he slowly trolled toward them. If he took a couple spaces no one would complain, in fact they'd probably assume that the car belonged to someone who worked at one of the stores.

He eased into a space beside a red pickup truck and turned off the motor. A light glaze of sweat glistened on his skin. Even with the air-conditioning running full blast, his grandmother's vehicle was a rolling greenhouse. Waiting for Morgan to appear in her car was out of the question. He glanced at his wristwatch. It was a few minutes before ten, and she should be here any time. He reached over and opened the door. He'd go back to the coffee shop and wait there until she appeared.

An hour and a half later, Frank jabbed the bottom of the plastic cup with the straw in a vain effort to break the remaining ice. A steady stream of people had come and gone from the store, but Morgan was still missing in action. He shifted in the chair and fingered the cup as he considered walking into the store to see if maybe he'd missed her arrival. He got up and dumped his cup into the trash.

He was about to pull the door open when a large black SUV cruised past the café window. Frank froze and stared at the driver. *Was it him, the man in the suit?* He walked down the length of the window and angled for a better view.

The man stepped out of the vehicle and surveyed the parking lot. Frank held his breath and waited. Oh yeah, it's him, Frank thought. His heart pounded. What's that they say? Fight or Flight? Right now, he couldn't do either. The driver had a don't-mess-with-me vibe about him which made the young man briefly rethink the wisdom of yesterday's notes and road-kill rabbit. The man in the suit looked like he would introduce Frank's face to the asphalt without as much as a moment's hesitation if he approached Morgan.

For a few moments, the man in the suit stared at the cafe. Frank instinctively stepped back from the window. Had he been seen? He quickly surveyed the side door and cobbled together an exit strategy should the man approach the café.

But the driver didn't, he turned and walked into the jewelry store. Frank exhaled and then grinned. Now he knew. Morgan was here.

***

Shawn entered the store and found it impossible to proceed through the showroom to the back offices. A crowd of people hovered over the counters and peered in the display cases jockeying for a glimpse of the items up for auction tomorrow night.

A diamond necklace sat front and center in the main display case circling the throat of a black velvet bust. A pair of sapphire and diamond earrings and the matching ring sat on each side vying for their share of attention from the shoppers.

At the request of a buxom blonde, Mary pulled out the ring and handed it to the customer who slid it on her finger.

"Ooh." She stretched out her arm and studied her hand. "It's like something you'd see at a Hollywood premiere, don't you agree?"

Shawn suppressed a grin. He'd give her that. The ring was definitely a red carpet piece.

"Would you like to see the matching earrings?" the older sales clerk asked.

"Yes, please." The blonde's voice had a "gimme, gimme, gimme" quality which reminded him of a child begging for an extra cookie. He watched Mary pull out the earrings and the client placed them to her ear. Then he noticed the other woman.

The two could not have been more different. The well-dressed older woman possessed a quiet elegance and she perused the cases with occasional glances over at the young blonde who preened before the mirror.

He fought the urge to smile as he watched the pair. One was arm candy who aspired to be a rich wife, the other simply was.

Mary acknowledged the older woman. "I'll be with you in a few minutes, Mrs. Moore."

"No problem," the older woman replied.

The blonde glanced over and irritation flitted across her face briefly as she turned back to the mirror.

Jealous? Yeah, you should be. She's got what you want, Shawn thought.

After several minutes, the buxom blonde surrendered the ring and earrings back to Mary.

"We'll see what happens tomorrow night," the young woman whispered.

"Good luck at the auction," Mary said.

After the blonde left, Mrs. Moore walked up to the counter and greeted Mary as an old friend. After a few minutes of inspecting the pieces, the older woman left.

Mary escorted Shawn back to the security door and punched the code to let him in.

"Are those two women regulars?"

"Mrs. Moore is. The other lady, I've not seen before," Mary replied.

"They both liked the earrings and the ring. A little competition would be a good thing."

The clerk smiled. "I'd bet on Mrs. Moore."

Shawn flashed a smile and chuckled. "So would I."

He made his way through the back door and worked his way back to Morgan's office. He stopped at her office door and studied her as she chatted on the phone. She appeared relaxed, upbeat and happy.

"Yes, it's better than we hoped for." Morgan said.

She glanced up, the smile on her face widened, and she gestured to him to enter.

"Don't worry." She paused, and he heard a man's voice on the other end of the line.

"Your room reservations are made. All you and mom must do is show up. Dad, Shawn's here, I've got to go. Love you, too."

Morgan set the handset down, jumped up and ran over and gave him a hug. Shawn's body stiffened and he took a deep breath at her full body contact. His arms hung at his sides but Morgan squeezed and he responded by closing his arms around her. Morgan pulled back and looked him in the eyes. A subtle flush rose in her cheeks as she wiggled out of his embrace.

"Sorry," she replied. She retreated to the desk.

I'm not, the little voice in Shawn's head chided. "What happened, did you win the lottery?"

"Better," Morgan said. "The internet auction is doing very well. Everything has a bid. In fact, if you add the monies up, we've already exceeded the total revenue from last year's fundraiser and we haven't auctioned off the jewelry yet."

"Congratulations. Have you told your dad? What did he say?"

"He's pleased. I mean, really pleased." She grabbed the computer's mouse. "Come on, check this out."

Shawn walked around the desk and stood over her shoulder as she clicked the refresh button.

"Look. The weekend getaway got two more bids."

He leaned over and studied the screen. He caught the subtle scent of lavender, and he savored it. It was the same fragrance she wore yesterday. The light clean floral scent suited her.

She scrolled over the items and then paused. "You know, some of these items have bids well above the retail price. That surprises me. I expected a little of that, but some of these bids are way over."

"It's for a good cause." Shawn said.

"Let's keep our fingers crossed that this continues." She twisted around and glanced up at him. "What have you been up to?"

"I've got some news on your stalker."

Morgan's upbeat mood evaporated and her eyes took on a wary expression. "Okay."

"The fingerprints on the bottle found at your house match the ones on your car. He's the same guy."

Morgan leaned back in her chair. "We still don't know who he is, right?"

"Not yet. But we can hope that something will turn up."

She fingered the hair away from her face. "The sooner the better, I don't know how much more of this I can take."

Shawn nodded. "Are your parents cool with the change in accommodations?"

"Yup, reservations made."

"Good. I'm bringing in Sabrina to assist with your security. She's the lady you met yesterday at the office."

"Okay, no problem."

"I'm going to put her in the suite with you tomorrow evening."

Morgan opened her mouth and then closed it without comment. She leaned forward in the chair, slid her hand over to the mouse and exited out of the auction site. She stared at the computer screen. She spoke in a flat controlled voice, "I'm confused. If my stalker is as dangerous as you think, why don't you want to be in the adjoining room?"

Shawn clenched his jaw. If he didn't know better, he'd think Morgan took the change in plans personally. He stepped back and walked around the desk. He needed to look her in the eyes, get control of the situation, *and to put some space between them.*

Morgan locked eyes with him. "Where will you be?"

"I'll be there. But maybe he'll make a move with only a woman bodyguard close to you."

"If he does, can Sabrina handle this?"

"I believe so. She's been trained for security detail, has several years of karate and I'll be there for back up."

"What color?" Morgan asked.

"Color," her question threw him off guard. "I don't know the color of the dress she'll wear."

Morgan smirked and then giggled. "No silly. What color belt is Sabrina at?"

Shawn paused, "Uh, not sure. Purple, I think. I haven't asked her recently."

"Not black?"

"She might be by now. You can ask her."

"I will," Morgan said.

CHAPTER 14

Shawn shot a glance over to Morgan as he pulled into the driveway at Copper Creek.

"Are you okay?"

"I'm fine, just had a déjà vu moment."

He didn't like the tone of her voice. A nervous quality threaded through it.

Shawn cruised past the visitor parking lot and stopped at the front entrance. A young man in uniform came around and took the keys from Shawn for the valet parking. Morgan waited as Shawn walked around and assisted her out of the car. He leaned down and whispered in her ear. "Let's see if we get any notes today."

Morgan glanced at him and murmured, "God, I hope not. The ones we received yesterday were more than enough for me."

Shawn slid his arm behind her and urged her to the front door. Morgan moved forward and by the time they reached the banquet manager's office, Ellen was waiting for them. "We're ready for the walk through." She escorted them to the ballroom and Shawn listened as Ellen and Morgan ticked off the final tasks with the timelines. The flowers arrived at two, the band sound check at three, bar set up at five, and the event launched at six. The time schedule rivaled a military campaign. He admired how Morgan rolled through the list without notes as she strolled around the ballroom and checked the layout.

Morgan took several minutes and walked the room before turning back to the employee and Shawn. "Ellen, this is perfect."

The banquet manager smiled and visibly relaxed. "Thank you. Copper Creek Resort is honored to be chosen this year as the location for the fundraiser. We hope the relocation of the event here will be the first of many years."

Shawn heard a buzzing sound and Ellen pulled up her pager to study the screen. "I'm sorry. I must take this. Is there anything else we need to cover?"

"No, we're good. Again, thank you," Morgan said.

Ellen left, and Shawn surveyed the empty display case at the front of the dining area. "You didn't discuss the plans on how to handle the jewelry."

"The resort is not involved," Morgan replied. "The pieces are coming via armored truck at five-thirty."

"Good." For a few moments he harbored the concern Morgan might personally bring them from the store and that added an element to the security he'd prefer not to deal with.

"I have a question for you." Morgan said.

He glanced over at her. "Shoot."

"How do you really feel about Mexican food?"

He snorted a laugh. "Why do you ask?"

"I noticed you ordered a burger for lunch at Lupe's."

Morgan walked over to him and flashed a mischievous grin. "Come on, dinner. Tonight, your place, I'll cook."

He grinned. "You don't have to. We can order pizza."

Her smirk bloomed into a full smile. "You don't think I can find my way around the kitchen, do you?"

Shawn arched his brows, cocked his head slightly, and grinned. "Can you?"

She gasped in a melodramatic fashion and broke into a throaty laugh before giving him a soft playful smack on the arm and taking a step back. "Yes, I can. But if you are scared that you won't survive the experience, we can order pizza."

"No, I trust you." Shawn reached out for her. Morgan stepped back and gave him a soft smile. Her eyes were golden brown and sparkled with warmth and promise. He sucked in a shallow breath at her silent invitation.

The little voice in his head whispered he shouldn't get emotionally involved, that doing this could go wrong in so many ways. But his chest tensed and his heart literally ached in protest.

"Well?" Morgan asked.

"Oh, what the hell," he pulled her in and kissed her.

Morgan melted into his arms and a soft whisper of a groan escaped her lips.

Memories of Christy and the past evaporated. All that mattered was here and now. He opened his lips and let his tongue gently tease her lips. Morgan opened to him and he deepened his kiss, savoring her softness and warmth.

When Morgan slid her hands around his neck he drew her in for full body contact. He felt the softness of her breasts against his chest, the way she gently stroked the nape of his neck and the way her tongue played against his. He drank in the sensations greedily, like a man who was dying of thirst and who'd just been given water.

Shawn pulled back and took a few fast draws of air. He needed to slow this down now, or they'd both end up on the carpet. Morgan opened her eyes and looked up at him through half-opened eyes simmering with desire.

The room divider behind her swayed and he did a quick double take. Not a little swing for the air conditioning hitting them, but seriously swinging back and forth. *What the… We're not alone.*

Morgan opened her eyes and frowned. "Shawn?"

She turned in the direction of his stare and then glanced back at him. He raised his finger to his lips, signaling for her to be silent as he walked over and yanked the dividers. They snapped violently against his pull but did not open.

"Stay here." Shawn passed her in long strides and opened the door to the room and scanned the hallway. *Empty.* He strode up to the adjoining ballroom door and paused to withdraw his gun. He slowly pulled the door open. He glanced from side to side before he entered and searched the room. No one was there. He holstered his weapon, walked over to the blinds and gave them a light touch. They moved slightly but lacked the swing he'd witnessed moments ago. Shawn then gave them a good firm shove. They swayed back and forth. Clearly someone had pushed them. Maybe an employee or was it someone else? *Like Morgan's stalker.* He'd never know. Whoever had been here was long gone. Shawn reached out and stilled the divider.

I let my guard down. The voice in his head chastised him. He wasn't supposed to get distracted. He put both Morgan and himself in jeopardy if he did. Shawn ran his hand through his hair and closed his eyes. He needed to get a grip on this, *on everything.*

"Morgan, are you okay?" Shawn asked.

Her reply was muffled by the divider. "I'm fine."

"Don't move. I'll be there in a minute." He turned and headed back to the Arizona Ballroom. As he entered the door, Morgan strode up to him. Her expression was a mix of worry and anticipation. "Well?"

"Nothing, come on, we're out of here."

He positioned himself at her side as they walked down the hallway and headed through the lobby to the front entrance. As they stood waiting for the valet to retrieve his SUV, Shawn glanced down at her. Morgan appeared perfectly calm, except for one dead giveaway, her hands. She fingered her purse restlessly.

"Mexican food for dinner, what did you have in mind?" He asked.

She glanced up at him with a moment of confusion flittering across her face. His question caught her off guard, but she forced a smile.

"Sour cream enchiladas."

***

Frank waited until they left for the parking lot before he sprinted to his car. The instant the engine fired, he cranked the air-conditioning up full blast. He'd found her. She'd been at the store. This time he wouldn't lose her.

A light sweat broke, and he took short rapid breaths. Frank wasn't sure whether it was the thrill of finding her or the hunt, but he was amped on a heady adrenaline buzz and had only one thought, get near Morgan. Frank craved her like an addict who needed his next fix.

He wrestled with the not-so-smart urge to catch up and follow more closely. But after yesterday, Frank knew he'd have to hang back. When the SUV turned west on Lincoln Drive, he grinned. They were driving to the resort. He slowed down below the speed limit, letting the gap between them widen. They would already be inside the hotel by the time he arrived and they wouldn't be any the wiser.

Frank pulled into the driveway of the resort and scanned the lot the couple used yesterday. The black SUV was nowhere to be found. His heart pounded rapidly as he detoured from the entrance and glided by the valet parking. *Where was their vehicle?* He clenched the steering wheel and forced himself to slow his car as he surveyed the parking lot. Tucked away in the back, he found the black Escalade.

Frank eased his grandmother's car to a stop. Where should he park? This vehicle would stick out like a sore thumb among the luxury automobiles. What he needed was somewhere out of the way. He lifted his foot off the brake pedal and crept forward. "I know," he murmured. "I'll use the employee parking lot."

Several minutes later he found the lot and after parking the car, Frank stepped out and glanced around. Three Hispanic women wearing maid uniforms stood outside the employee entrance speaking in animated tones. He didn't understand Spanish and avoided eye contact as he strode past them. Laughter erupted and he stiffened before taking a quick glance over his shoulder at the maids. They weren't looking at him, or worse, laughing at him.

Frank opened the door and stepped in. The light glaze of sweat super cooled him as he moved down the hallway. A shiver of anticipation reverberated through him as he narrowed his hunt for the couple. Few people were out this time of the day. He passed the restaurant, gift shop, and lobby and no one gave him a second glance as he strode toward the wing where the ballrooms were located. As he reached his destination, he stopped at the mirror that hung on the wall. His heart thudded rapidly, and he wiped his palms on the sides of his chino pants.

He studied his reflection for a few seconds before finger combing his dark brown hair back and adjusting his oxford shirt. He looked okay. No one would think he didn't belong here. Stealing a quick glance around the corner, he checked the hallway before he jogged down to the Arizona Ballroom's doors. As he reached for them, he froze.

What was he doing? This wasn't the plan. Their first face-to-face meeting was supposed to take place alone. No distractions or competition from anyone. Morgan needed to know how much he cared for her. He should leave and stick to his plan, but he couldn't. The voice inside his mind screamed at him to get closer.

He walked a few doors down and cracked open the door to the adjoining ballroom and peeked in. The sunlight filtered through the sheer drapes giving the impression of a cloudy day. The expanse of wheat-colored carpeting, barren of any chairs or tables, made the room appear huge.

He slipped in and crept up to the room dividers. The conversation on the other side was in low quiet tones. Morgan said something about Mexican food and the man said something about pizza. Now the voices stopped. Without thinking, Frank placed his hands on the divider and leaned in to hear.

The temporary wall rolled away from him. He lurched back before attempting to stop the movement. The few seconds of swaying seemed like an eternity. When the dividers stopped swinging, he exhaled a ragged breath. Had they noticed? Frank touched the screen with his fingers. The room next door was silent. Then the dividers jerked violently.

Frank jumped back, almost stumbling and falling on his butt. *Shit!* He scrambled to his feet, and the adrenaline turned his knees to rubber. He staggered a few steps and then bolted to the exit. He hit the door, shoving it wide open before he sprinted down the hallway. Only after he reached the main building did he slow to a walk. He paused and glanced over his shoulder to confirm he wasn't followed. He studied the guest traffic around the lobby. They were preoccupied by their own affairs. He smirked, and a nervous giggle erupted as he shoved his hands in his pockets and strolled back to his car.

He started up the engine, stretched over to turn up the air-conditioning to maximum, and waited for the valet to retrieve their vehicle. Sweat pooled into tears which traveled down his face, chest, and back.

"I'm sweating like a stuck pig."

Frank wiped his sleeve across his brow and then tapped his fingers on the steering wheel. Within a few minutes, a valet appeared and retrieved the Escalade. Frank tightened his grip. They wouldn't give him the slip this time.

He turned on the radio and tuned in his favorite station. The heavy metal music pulsed through the speakers, and caused the dashboard to vibrate in rhythm to the song. He waited until he glimpsed the SUV head back to the main road, then he shifted the car in gear and followed.

The Escalade reached Scottsdale Road and made a left turn heading north. Were they going back to the store or were they heading somewhere else? He wrestled the impulse to move in closer. He'd been stupid yesterday because he followed too closely. To do this right you have to hang back, fade into the background, like "white noise", and he could do that. Frank was the poster boy for white noise.

When they passed Shea Road, they made a turn into a shopping center and went into a grocery store. Frank toyed with the idea of waiting in the car for them to come out but the air-conditioning in his grandmother's car was mediocre at best. He parked a few rows over and followed them inside. Frank grasped a shopping cart and trolled down the aisles casting quick glances searching for them. He found them pulling cans off the shelf in the Mexican food section.

Morgan was placing items into a shopping cart while the man stood nearby. The man said something in a low voice Frankie couldn't make out. Probably a joke because Morgan looked up at him and laughed before setting a few items in the cart. They looked like they belonged together, and the realization struck Frankie in the gut like he'd been sucker punched. He held his breath and clenched the shopping cart. *No, this can't be. Morgan and I are meant to be together.*

He began to draw rapid breaths as his anger boiled. He had to get out of here, now, before he did something really stupid. He rolled the cart away a few feet before he abandoned it and walked briskly back to the car.

He reached the vehicle, stopped and looked around. What was he going to do now?

Transparent waves of heat rippled over the dark asphalt of the parking lot. He spied them at the store entrance. *Here they come.*

Morgan and the man placed their groceries in the back of the SUV. The man never strayed far from Morgan's side. Hell, he even opened the passenger door for her to slide in. Who did that anymore? "Sorry dude, but things are about to change. Nothing you can do or say is going to change that," Frankie murmured.

The Escalade pulled out of the parking lot and headed north on Scottsdale road. Frank put the car in reverse and followed. He wouldn't lose them this time. In fact, the longer he trailed them, the more he began to believe he had a talent for tracking people. This SUV worked its way through the late afternoon traffic for another twenty minutes when it happened. Frank missed clearing the intersection during the same light as the SUV.

He sat in front of a line of cars and stared in frustration as the distance between them increased. Frank squirmed in his seat and glanced left and right as he pondered running the red light. The smaller the SUV became, the more nervous he became. "God, don't let me lose them now."

Just when Frank though he'd lost them, the SUV pulled into a left turn lane and entered Kierland Commons.

"Now what?" Frank muttered as they disappeared from sight.

The light changed green and he floor boarded the gas pedal. He had to catch them. Not bothering to use the signals, he careened across the lanes to reach the turn lane. He squeezed the steering wheel while he waited for a break in traffic.

He'd barely entered the main street to the mall when he glimpsed the SUV make a right turn down a side street several blocks up. Frank slowed his vehicle to a crawl until he reached the four way stop where they had turned.

Should he follow? What if he had to get away quickly? He craned his neck around hoping to get a clear view of what he would drive into, but couldn't see much.

"Hell," he growled as he turned the steering wheel and proceeded down the side street. Within seconds, the street dead ended into a large parking lot. Most of the spaces had been cordoned off for restaurant valet parking.

"Blood suckers. Isn't there anywhere in Scottsdale where you can park for free?" Frank mumbled a curse as he navigated the large vehicle, searching for free spaces. Finding a small cache of unreserved spaces at the back of the lot, he eased his car into one and turned off the motor. Now he'd find them.

He stepped out and scanned the lot for their vehicle. Most of the cars were expensive European imports and the occasional Hummer, so he walked across the lot and doubled back along the side street. Where had they gone? He spied an entrance to a subterranean parking garage. The words "tenant parking" discretely marked the entrance. He quickly looked around to confirm no one was watching and then stepped inside.

Several seconds passed before his eyes adjusted to the cool darkness. The cavernous space echoed every sound. His tennis shoes made a soft padding sound on the concrete floor. Frank walked cautiously, trying to be as quiet as possible and praying he wouldn't run into a security guard. Then he walked around and proceeded up the ramp to the second floor. There, he found what he was looking for: the black Escalade.

He walked over and peered in the tinted windows. Of course Morgan wasn't there, but had she left anything behind? He scanned the empty interior of the vehicle. Nothing.

Stinking transmitter, he'd paid a small fortune for it and it didn't work. "I'm going to get a refund," Frank whispered as he bent over and reached inside the wheel well. His fingers felt the warm metal of the truck and he chewed on his lip while he groped and searched for it.

A car came up the ramp and headed toward him. Frank crouched down and crawled around to hide behind the front bumper. The white BMW cruised by and parked several spaces down. He didn't move as the engine shut off, and someone stepped out of the car. He slowly straightened up, and peered over the cars when the sound of retreating footsteps assured him they weren't walking toward him.

A man in a suit walked over to the elevator at the far end of the garage. He inserted a pass key and stepped inside before the doors closed.

Frank walked over. All he found was a brass plate with the words "The Vistas". "Damn!" He slapped the elevator door and stood back, half hoping they'd open for him. Somewhere up among the expensive, exclusive, and password protected condominiums was Morgan.

He stormed out of the garage. So close! He turned right as he exited the entrance and strode toward the main street, looking up every few seconds at the building he couldn't get into.

His mind ticked off questions to which he had no answers. How would he get in? Which condo? What was she doing? No. Don't think about that. Desperation morphed into a rage as images of Morgan with the man entered his mind. They were up there together.

Frank crossed the courtyard and took a seat in front of the man-made water geysers. A few families had brought their children to play in the water. He stared across the street at the tower. How was he going to find her?

Fire escape? There must be stairs which ended on the ground floor. But even if he found them, he had no idea where to go from there.

Screams of laughter caught his attention, and he gazed at the children as they cavorted around. A father and mother sat on a bench and laughed at the antics. His resentment bubbled.

Whether it was God, fate, or simply bad Karma, he'd never know, but these kids had something he never had, a family. His father had skipped on him and his mom so long ago that Frank had no clear memory of him. His mother had never been around much either. She either worked or spent her time searching for the next Mr. Right in all the wrong places.

There had been a succession of men after his old man left. His mother told him to call them uncles, but they weren't. Sometimes nice, sometimes not, for the most part they were indifferent to him. To them, Frank was like furniture, something they had to navigate around and avoid bumping into.

His eyes traveled back to the condos. He must get to Morgan.

CHAPTER 15

Morgan set the groceries on the counter and walked over to the patio door. She gazed at the sky as dusk settled. This was her favorite time of the day. The summer sun worked nothing short of a miracle when evening came to the Arizona desert. The neutral palette of beige and sun-bleached green transformed into rich tones. Like a kaleidoscope wheel, the colors flowed from sky blue to yellow, orange, red and finally faded to dusty purple before the darkness settled in.

Shawn unpacked the food in the kitchen, and she heard the rustle of grocery bags. If she didn't get dinner started they'd be eating later than she'd like, so she went to change into jeans and a top. By the time she returned to the kitchen, Shawn had finished putting the groceries away and taken a beer out of the fridge.

"Want one?"

"Thanks," she replied. He pulled another bottle out, removed the cap, and handed it to her. "I've never made sour cream enchiladas before."

Morgan took a sip. "You don't have to help. Go sit and relax."

He went around and sat down on the bar stool on the other side of the counter. "Tell me more about you and Brad."

She did her best not to cringe when he mentioned her ex-boyfriend's name. She knew the topic would come up eventually. Yesterday's phone conversation with Brad had been a virtual slap in the face and left no room for doubt that things were over.

Until now, she had avoided talking about the breakup with anyone. But in the wake of last night's talk with Shawn about his failed relationship, she couldn't refuse to answer.

Morgan stalled as she took the rotisserie chicken out of the plastic container, removed the skin and pulled the meat from the bones. She sensed his gaze on her and ignored him as she continued to work on the chicken. "I'm not sure where to start. Exactly what do you want to know?"

"Let's start with something simple. How did you two meet?"

"We met through a mutual friend two years ago." Morgan said.

"Stella introduced you?"

"No, my friend Liz did." Morgan paused and glanced up at Shawn. His face was expressionless, and she couldn't get a beat on what he was thinking. Morgan resumed pulling the meat off the chicken. "Brad and I had been exclusive for about a year."

"Sounded serious," Shawn said.

Morgan set the chicken into a small bowl, washed the cutting board, and then picked up the onion. She sliced off both ends and peeled away the brown papery skin.

"Yeah," she replied. "At least I thought so."

"What happened?"

Morgan's eyes watered as she stacked the slices and cut them into small pieces. *Well, at least I can blame the tears on the onion.* She finished and scooped the diced onion into another small bowl. Then she rinsed the knife and took a sip from her beer.

Shawn sat in silence and watched her. At first look, she would've thought he was calm and detached, but his finger steadily worked at peeling the label from the bottle. "He didn't want to take the next step. I guess in the end we wanted different things," she replied.

Shawn studied her. "Was the break up bad?"

"No. There wasn't a fight or an argument. We just went our own ways. I guess you can call it mutual."

He set the bottle down and looked down at the remains of the beer's label which littered the granite countertop. "I don't believe in mutual. Someone always walks away first."

Morgan didn't reply immediately. She'd never thought of it that way, but Shawn had a point. After they had "the talk", Brad became elusive. *He'd walked away first.* She nodded. "You may be right. Where's the can opener?"

"Second drawer from the top on your left," Shawn replied.

Morgan began to open the cans of cream, chicken soup and diced green chilies. "We wanted different things."

"Yeah, I understand how that happens."

Morgan glanced up at him. There was no pity in his eyes, only empathy, an all-too-familiar solidarity shared by those who'd been walked away from. "I need something to mix up the sauce in."

"The large cabinet behind you."

She turned, opened the door, and searched before pulling out a large plastic bowl. She added the sour cream, soup, and green chilies, and stirred them before turning the oven on. Morgan then arranged the tortillas, cheese, chicken, and sauce near a casserole dish she found when she searched for the mixing bowl.

Morgan glanced down. An array of ingredients lay around her. "Now comes the easy part, filling and rolling the tortillas."

Shawn set down his beer on the counter. "Let me help."

He got up from the bar stool and came into the kitchen, washed his hands, and then stood next to her. "Where do I start?"

Morgan smiled and explained the process of loading the tortillas and filling the casserole dish. She grinned. "You're not off the hook. You owe me pancakes, remember?"

"Tomorrow," Shawn said.

"Promise?"

"Cross my heart and hope to die."

***

He should feel nervous. Morgan had gone domestic goddess on him. Making dinner at his place was the type of thing a long-term girlfriend might do, not someone you met less than two days ago, and certainly not a client. The speed at which things were progressing would make almost any normal red-blooded American male freak out. Hell, he should be running for the hills; instead here he was, standing in his kitchen helping her prepare dinner and feeling good about it.

After the casserole dish went into the oven, Shawn pulled a second beer from the fridge and retreated to the living room where he sank into a leather recliner and turned on the flat screen TV. The cable news channel recapped the day's major events while sound bite news items scrolled along the bottom in ticker tape fashion. Shawn stared at the screen and pretended to watch while his mind processed what she'd said.

He'd been a bit ruthless in probing about her relationship with Brad. Had Morgan kicked back, he would have countered that her ex-boyfriend might be connected with her stalker. But, for some reason he couldn't clearly define, he needed to know how committed the relationship had been, and why they'd broken up.

Morgan had surprised him with her honest admission that she'd been ready to settle down, and Brad hadn't. The good old biological clock, it was as simple as that. Most men eventually would have to deal with the use-it-or-lose-it fertility issue when it came to the women they dated long term. In his experience, most women in their late twenties heeded the clock's call. He cast a glance over at Morgan as she pulled plates and silverware from the cabinet and came around to set the dinner table.

"You're staring," she said quietly.

The evening shadow placed the dining room area in darkness and the lights over the dining room table were off, so Shawn couldn't read her face, but he detected a touch of amusement in her voice.

He shifted his gaze back to the TV and took another swallow from his beer.

"What do you want to drink with dinner, iced tea?" Morgan asked.

"Tea's fine. How long do the enchiladas need to cook?"

"Not long, maybe another twenty minutes."

Shawn picked up the remote control and switched channels to ESPN. He glanced back at Morgan as she added tortilla chips to a bowl and salsa to another before bringing them to the table.

His eyes shifted back to the TV screen. He didn't want to get caught watching her again.

After she finished in the kitchen Morgan came and sat down on the sofa. She sipped the beer and announced, "Since we're checking in to the resort tomorrow, I'll think I'll pack tonight."

A soft tremor of regret rippled through him as a battle raged between his brain and his gut. *I shouldn't have brought her here in the first place. This is inevitable, even necessary.*

He looked at Morgan. She was all coolness and courtesy. What a contrast from the temptress he kissed this afternoon. Was she battling the same emotions that he was but better at hiding it? "When do we need to be at the hotel tomorrow?" He asked.

Morgan took another sip of her beer. "Check in is at two. I'd like to go over at noon, do one final walk through, then see if I can squeeze a manicure in at the spa."

He nodded. "I'll have Sabrina be there at eleven thirty. She'll escort you on your rounds tomorrow."

"Where will you be?"

He took a deep breath and exhaled slowly. "I'll be around." *Just in case.*

A troubled expression floated across her face. He left the recliner and joined her on the sofa. She took a slow ragged breath, reached for his hand, and threaded her fingers through his. The simplicity of her gesture made his chest tighten, and he wrapped his fingers around hers. "Morgan, I'll be there for you. But maybe if I pull back, he'll make his move, and we'll catch him."

He shifted his body to angle hers and looked into her eyes. Morgan's eyes watered, and she gulped, "I know."

"I believe this thing with your stalker will resolve itself soon. Then you'll have your life back."

She nodded, took a deep breath, and bit her lip. "I hope when this is over..."

He didn't let her finish. He leaned down and kissed her. Morgan untangled her fingers and snaked her arms around his neck. Her lips were soft, and she had the faint taste of beer on her. He cupped his hand to her cheek and deepened his kiss as she shimmied closer.

The soft trill of the oven timer went off behind them. For a fraction of a second Shawn thought he imagined the sound. Morgan pulled back and gave a soft throaty giggle. "Dinner is served."

Shawn nodded and sat back. Morgan stood up and walked to the kitchen. Isolation and a chill enrobed him. Then Shawn knew. The end of this case would signal a new beginning.

***

Morgan placed the last of her makeup in the tote. Shawn had already taken the garment bag with the evening gown and her large suitcase down to the SUV.

The Internet auction bids would bring more than enough funds to make the fundraiser an unqualified success; however she wouldn't feel completely out of the woods until tonight was over. She surveyed the loft, doing a visual once over to check that she didn't leave anything.

The light in the kitchen was on. She stepped over and flipped the switch off as Shawn came in and picked up her tote bag.

"Ready?" He asked.

"Yes, let's go."

They walked down the hall in silence, and as they reached the elevator, Morgan's phone chimed. She glanced at the caller ID. "It's my parent's home line."

"Go ahead and answer," Shawn replied as they stepped in and traveled down in the elevator.

"Hi."

"How are things going?" Her mother asked.

"Can't complain. I checked the auction this morning and we're doing well, absolutely no problems."

"Morgan, Vicki's coming."

"Fantastic." Her younger sister had been in Mexico working on an archeological dig and hadn't been sure she would be back in town in time for the event.

"Where's she staying?"

"We got her a room. She's flying back the day after tomorrow."

"So soon? I wanted more time to visit with her."

"So do your father and I," her mother replied. "Perhaps you can talk her into staying longer. Any new developments?"

Morgan immediately picked up the concern in her mother's voice and sought to assure her. "No. Things have been quiet."

"Maybe he's gone," her mother added hopefully.

Morgan didn't want to upset her mother, so she replied evasively. "Time will tell."

She cast a quick glance over at Shawn who gave her a sharp look. He overheard her side of the conversation and had managed to put the pieces together. They walked out of the elevator and across the underground garage to his SUV. The phone's reception became scratchy.

"Mom, you're cutting out. I'll check in later."

Shawn pushed the unlock button as the SUV chirped and the lights flashed. He walked her around to the passenger side and held the door for her to slide in. Morgan wondered if Shawn's plan of pulling back and baiting her stalker would work.

She couldn't keep him in her employ forever, and her stalker had been quiet, or at least not destructive, in the past twenty-four hours. Perhaps her mother had a point, and her stalker had given up?

Shawn slid in and started the engine.

"You'll get to meet my sister tonight, Vicki's coming."

"How long is she staying?"

"She'll be leaving the day after tomorrow. She came in only for the fundraiser."

"Has she heard about your stalker?"

"I don't know. Maybe my parents told her."

"I'm looking forward to meeting her."

Morgan smiled and glanced out the passenger side window as they left the parking garage. Her sister was a shrewd judge of people. In Morgan's experience, no one could size things up quicker and put the puzzle pieces together faster than Vicki. Her sister's appraisal of the situation would be valuable.

CHAPTER 16

Shawn pulled the SUV up to the resort's front entrance and turned the motor off. As the staff took the luggage, he canvassed the parking lot. A slight adrenaline buzz hummed through him as if he were on deck and next to bat in a baseball game.

He and Morgan entered the lobby and found Sabrina standing against the wall across from the front desk. He studied her and frowned. She looked nervous. Not terrified, just fidgety what-the-hell-am-I doing-here nervous. Sabrina saw him, and she forced a smile.

Morgan recognized her, walked up, and extended her hand. "Hi. I understand you're my new best friend."

Sabrina grinned. "Let's hope by the end of today you won't kick me to the curb."

Morgan's smile faded. "Why would I do that?"

Sabrina blushed and began to fidget with her fingers. "What I mean is you don't grow tired of me escorting you everywhere."

"I'm sure we'll get along famously," Morgan replied.

Shawn spoke up, "Let's get the luggage into the rooms and firm up the game plan for today and this evening."

Morgan glanced at him and annoyance briefly graced her face, "Fine."

She turned and walked toward the check-in desk leaving Shawn and Sabrina standing together. Sabrina looked up at Shawn with a puzzled expression before she picked up her tote bag and followed behind Morgan.

Shawn soon discovered one of the major perks of being the patron of a charity fundraiser is that you get to check into the hotel early and with a level of speed which left him speechless. The staff treated Morgan like a celebrity. No waiting in line, a bellboy appeared out of thin air to collect the luggage, and within minutes they were on the way to their rooms.

As Morgan walked alongside the bellboy, Sabrina trailed a few steps behind looking around like Dorothy when she landed in Oz. Shawn pressed his lips together; had he made a mistake asking for the young woman to provide back up on this case? Shawn didn't know much about Sabrina, but she was acting as if she had never been at a resort before. He caught up and gently pulled her arm, so she turned to face him.

"What's going on? Are you okay?"

"Nothing," she replied. "I'm fine."

He leaned over Sabrina and growled, "Are you sure?"

Sabrina eyes widened, and she started to step back from him. Suddenly, she checked herself, straightened up, and looked him directly in the eyes. "Yeah, I'm sure."

Shawn smirked and nodded. "Good. Look, your job is simple. Morgan is running the event. She has a schedule of things to do today. All you have to do is be near and make sure that her stalker doesn't get to her. Don't get distracted. We're her bodyguards. You saw the video footage and know what to watch for. This event is a perfect opportunity for him to try to get to her. I'm hoping with you by her side, we might bait him into action."

He stared into her eyes. She nodded as his words sank in. "It's a job," she whispered.

"That's right," Shawn replied.

Shawn let go of her arm and stepped back. Sabrina jogged to catch up with Morgan. After a few yards she stopped and glanced back at him. She cracked a mischievous grin as she mouthed, "A really cool job." He grinned at her, and before he could reply, she spun and hurried to catch up with Morgan.

***

Morgan was slightly surprised when the bellboy opened the door. Sabrina quietly spoke up and asked to go in first. She stepped aside and waited as the petite woman walked in and disappeared for several minutes. Morgan glanced over at Shawn. He stood nearby and made no comment. He had changed from last night. Here stood the cool, no nonsense man she encountered when they first met. *He's expecting something to happen.* A shiver rippled through her, but before she could speak, Sabrina reappeared and gestured for her to come in.

Morgan looked at the young woman as she walked into her suite. What a major change from the nervous young woman in the lobby. Shawn had spoken to her in the hallway and Morgan walked on ahead, letting them talk in private. Whatever Shawn had said must've made a big impression because the nervous girl from the lobby was gone.

The living room was decorated in soft earth tones and on each side sat a bedroom. Morgan directed the bellboy to put her luggage in the room on the right. "Let's take a few minutes to unpack, and we'll meet back here."

Sabrina nodded and turned to the bedroom on the other side. Morgan had barely finished removing the evening gown from the garment bag and unloading the tote bag in the bathroom when she heard a knock on the front door. She went to the living room to find that Sabrina had let Shawn in.

He entered the room and gestured to her to sit down with Sabrina. "Okay, give us your itinerary."

Morgan paused briefly and collected her thoughts. "Well, the flowers will arrive at two. My parents should also arrive around then. I expect my father will want to go see the ballroom first thing. Band has a sound check at three. The jewelry will be coming in around 5:30. I must be there to receive the shipment and set things up. My schedule is open for the next two hours and I was hoping to squeeze a quick manicure in at the spa."

Shawn looked at Sabrina. "You go with her this afternoon to the salon and on her rounds. I'll be present when the jewelry arrives. In the meantime, I'm hanging back. When your parents and sister arrive, inform me. I'll check on them periodically."

Morgan's stomach tightened into a knot at Shawn's last comment. "Do you think my family is at risk?"

He shook his head. "Probably not, but I want to keep an eye on them just to be safe."

She studied his face, trying to read him. Was he telling the truth or hiding his concerns from her? He caught her staring and his lips crooked into a small smile. "Morgan, don't worry, they'll be safe."

"Sabrina, you're up." With that comment, Shawn stood up and gave them both a final glance and left. Morgan sat and watched. She half-expected he'd turn around and say something or just give her a small smile, but he didn't. She took a slow deep breath while she mentally sorted out what to make of his change of attitude.

Sabrina asked, "Did you make an appointment at the spa or can we walk-in?"

"What?" Morgan replied, as she turned her gaze from the door to her female bodyguard.

"Your manicure, can we just show up?"

"I haven't made an appointment. Let me call."

A few minutes later, Morgan found out the salon could take them in twenty minutes. She found Sabrina unpacking her toiletries and clothing.

Morgan paused at the door as Sabrina hung up her outfit in the closet. The lady traveled light, too light. No evening gown, just a simple pantsuit, all in black. Morgan was about to speak and then stopped. Sabrina was here to protect her. The black pantsuit, while not elegant, was a practical choice.

"I'm ready to head down," she announced quietly.

Sabrina closed the closet door, grabbed her cell phone and the room card before she slipped on a denim blazer.

"You're not armed."

Sabrina smiled. "Don't need to be."

"Shawn said you had taken martial arts."

"Yeah, I teach a women's self-defense class too."

"Can you show me a few moves?" Morgan asked.

"Sure, later this afternoon if you've got time."

They left and walked to the elevator. "How long have you been working for Sonoran Security?"

Sabrina glanced back at Morgan after she had scanned the hallway, "About a year and a half. I started doing event security part-time. The pay was good compared to waitressing at my parents restaurant, so when the chance came up to go full-time, I took it."

Morgan nodded. "Working in family businesses can be challenging at times."

Sabrina punched the button to summon the elevator. "That's an understatement. My family owns a restaurant on the Westside. My parents started it shortly after they got married." Sabrina's eyes scanned the elegant wallpaper and sconces that decorated the hallway. "It's not big or fancy, but they do well enough to raise a family with it."

No wonder she looked nervous when we arrived. A resort like this is a whole new experience for her. "You know, most start-up businesses fail, so you must be proud of your parent's success. It's quite an accomplishment."

The young raven-haired woman looked at Morgan. Sabrina studied her dress, her expensive handbag, and shoes. "Yeah, I am. It's great to work with family, but I needed to do something on my own."

"You and my sister Vicki, she decided working in the family business wasn't for her either."

The elevator door opened, and they stepped in. Morgan pushed the button for the first floor.

"Did you know the salon here is first rate?" Morgan asked. "You can get a massage, manicures, pedicures, facials, hair styling and even have them do your make-up if you wish." She glanced over to Sabrina to gauge her reaction.

"Are you planning on having more than a manicure?" Sabrina asked.

"I'm thinking about letting them do my hair and make-up. Were you going to do something special with your hair tonight?"

Sabrina stared up at her with a stunned expression which quickly melted into a red flush and Morgan touched the young woman's arm.

"Sabrina, I'm sorry. I'm an idiot. I wasn't suggesting anything is wrong. You have beautiful hair, and I thought you might enjoy having it styled at the salon as my treat."

Sabrina's expression softened as she considered the offer. "I'm not sure I should."

"Why not?" Morgan asked.

"Shawn might think that I'm not guarding you."

"We can probably get stylist chairs side-by-side if we ask. We'll be together in the salon, how about that?"

Sabrina nibbled her lip then nodded. "That should be okay."

Morgan chuckled. "See, I told you we would get along."

***

"We were getting worried," William Kennedy announced as Sabrina and Morgan entered the Arizona ballroom.

Morgan flashed a smile at her parents. The spa had taken a little longer than planned and she was late. Shawn studied her and then glanced over at Sabrina. For a brief moment, Morgan thought she detected disapproval in his eyes.

"Were there any problems?" Shawn asked.

"No," Sabrina replied.

"Mom and Dad, I'd like to introduce you to Sabrina. She is part of the team with Sonoran Security and will be on duty with me tonight."

Morgan's mother smiled and extended her hand. "A pleasure to meet you."

Her father stood back and didn't comment. He was sizing up Sabrina, literally. His skeptical expression made it clear what he thought about Sabrina's ability to protect his daughter.

"Dad, Sabrina's been with Sonoran for over a year and a half, possesses a black belt in karate, and teaches women's self-defense classes."

William gave his daughter a nod and stepped forward extending his hand. Sabrina shook it, and to her credit, ignored his doubtful expression.

The room went awkwardly silent, and Morgan uttered a silent prayer of thanks when her mother spoke. "The room is absolutely lovely, dear."

"Thanks. The flower arrangements turned out beautiful, didn't they?"

"They're perfect," her mother said.

Shawn spoke up. "The musicians will be here in thirty minutes for set up and sound check. I'll stay. The jewelry is scheduled for five-thirty, right?"

"Yes," Morgan replied. "I must be back here to receive the shipment. There'll be two security guards with the display all evening."

"Sounds like a plan," William answered. "We'll retire to our room and rendezvous back down here later."

Shawn spoke up after her parents left the room. "Morgan, you better head back to your room too. You'll be safer there."

She sighed. She felt as if he was pushing her away, and there was little she could do. "Okay, call me if you find any problems."

She turned and headed out of the ballroom with Sabrina at her side. Once in the hotel suite Morgan went to her bedroom, closed the door and plopped down in the chair by the desk. She was exhausted mentally, physically, and emotionally.

She wished she could turn off the lights, crawl under the bed comforters, and sleep nonstop for the next couple of days. No fundraisers, store, or stalker. Morgan glanced down at her watch. She had to be downstairs in approximately two hours and all she could do is wait. There was a soft knock at the door. Morgan closed her eyes and leaned back in the chair. "Yes," she answered.

"Morgan, there is a woman at the front door who says her name is Victoria. She claims to be your sister."

"Thank God," Morgan murmured as she jumped out of the chair and left the bedroom. "Let her in."

Vicki stepped in the room. "Hey, how's it going?"

"It's going."

"You want to talk?"

Morgan reached out and hugged her sister. It had been so long since she had an opportunity to have a chat with Vicki. Oh how Morgan had missed her. Her sister was the one person who understood the pressure and challenges which came with dealing with her father, running the store and fundraiser. She ushered her sister into her bedroom, and Morgan shut the door while Vicki flopped on the bed.

"So, tell me about this stalker?"

Morgan sat down in the chair and recapped all that had happened within the last forty-eight hours while Vicki listened in silence. Only after Morgan had run out of words did she speak.

"It's about time," her sister murmured. "All I can say is good riddance."

"Vicki, what are you talking about?"

"Brad, he's out of the picture, and I say hasta la vista."

"Geez Vicki. He's the least of my problems right now," Morgan said.

"Yeah I know, but personally, I'm relieved you two have parted. He wasn't right for you."

Morgan eyed her sister. Vicki looked back at her unapologetically. "You always appeared to be working at it."

"Come on Vic," Morgan said.

"The guy was Mr. Perfect, never a hair out of place. Don't tell me that he wasn't high maintenance."

Morgan sat in silence as what her sister said sank in. "You're wrong. It wasn't like that. What we had was special."

Vicki leveled a stare at her. "Special? If Brad cared as deeply for you as you thought why hasn't he come crawling back?"

Her sister had a point. She leaned her head back on the chair while she closed her eyes. "Tell me Vicki, is it me or is it a guy thing?"

Vicki laughed softly. "Neither. It's a Brad thing."

"What am I going to do?"

"That's the easy part. All the hard work on this event is done. You're going to get dressed and swing by my room on your way down to pick me up. Tonight, I'm going to be your wingman, and you're going to have some fun. It's my mission to ensure you do. Don't worry about tomorrow. Deal with it…" her younger sister paused and gestured in the air with her arms, "tomorrow".

Morgan smiled, "Wingman?"

"Okay, wingwoman."

Morgan mulled over her sister's words. Take things one day at a time. "Vic, how did you get to be so smart?"

"According to the shaman down in Mexico, I'm an old soul."

Morgan gazed at her sister. "You're seeing a shaman?"

Vicki got off the bed and tugged down her blouse. "No, but when you work on archeological sites you have to make sure you don't piss off the locals. We had a local holy man come and sort of bless the site so the spirits would not be upset when we started the dig."

"I can't believe you did that. You, little miss scientist, giving into superstition."

Her younger sister looked up and crooked a grin. "Yeah, kinda strange, isn't it? I don't believe in curses or stuff like that, but having the shaman perform an offering was like having a bowl of chicken soup, it won't hurt."

Morgan laughed.

***

Shawn came down fifteen minutes ahead of when the guards were scheduled to arrive with the jewelry and found not only Morgan and Sabrina but a third woman he had never seen before.

Morgan wore a dark forest green evening gown and the other woman wore a short black cocktail dress. As he walked up to the trio, she studied him with interest.

Morgan piped up, "Shawn, this is my sister, Victoria."

The woman extended her hand to shake his. "Call me Vicki."

"Nice to meet you, I understand you flew in especially for the evening."

"I wouldn't miss this for the world. Morgan tells me you've done a lot of security work in California."

"Yes."

"Are you pulling back tonight in an effort to bait Morgan's stalker into making his move?"

He paused and then smiled. "That obvious, huh?"

Vicki nodded but concern floated behind her upbeat demeanor. "Do you think he'll surface soon?"

Shawn studied Morgan's sister. She had a calm but interested expression on her face. "Hard to say. Two days ago, I thought he was almost panicky with the notes and the vandalism. Since then he's been quiet." *Too quiet.*

Morgan's cell phone chimed. She answered it and spoke a few brief words before ending her conversation. "The jewelry's here."

Within minutes, two armed guards appeared at the door. Morgan opened the package, inspected the jewelry and signed the paperwork before they walked up to the case at the front of the ballroom. Morgan took the next couple of minutes to set up the pieces on display.

Shawn glanced over and noted Sabrina stood near Morgan, though not too close. Then as if the young female bodyguard sensed he was watching her, she made eye contact. He nodded in approval.

"Where will you be tonight?" Vicki asked.

"I'll be moving around the room."

"So you won't be enjoying the dinner?"

He grinned. "I wish. Sabrina and I are on duty. We'll order something from room service after the evening."

"Pity, this is going to be a long night."

The bartender had arrived to set up the bar, and the wait staff started setting up the utensils for the hors d' oeuvres. He glanced at Vicki. "If you would excuse me."

"Of course," she said.

Shawn headed over to the bar and after talking with the bartender, he crossed him off the list of potential problems. He had a wife and two children at home and moonlighted for extra money. No stalker potential there.

As Morgan's parents arrived, he followed a waiter through the side door and back into the kitchen. Morgan's sister was right, this was going to be a long night.

CHAPTER 17

Morgan stood at the front entrance to the ballroom with her parents and sister. She scanned the crowd of people who stood patiently waiting to enter, and pressed her lips together. She hated the reception line. This long-standing tradition, which her father insisted upon, meant the family personally greeted each of the guests. William Kennedy refused to accept today's custom which dictated a staged entrance where everyone stopped to be photographed like they were celebrities on the red carpet at an awards show. Morgan took a slow breath and prepared to shake the hands of the next couple. She'd been successful with introducing the Internet auction. Maybe next year she could get him to revisit the idea of eliminating the reception line.

"How are you doing?" The low familiar voice made her heart skip a beat. Morgan glanced up. Brad stood there looking handsome in his dark blue suit. She gulped and forced a smile.

"Brad, I'm fine. How are you?" Morgan leaned over and gave him a perfunctory peck of the cheek as a greeting.

"I' m doing great. Let me introduce Ashley."

Morgan turned and gazed upon her ex-boyfriend's date. A petite blonde smiled at her and Morgan instantly hoped no one noticed her shock. Ashley wore a blue evening gown which show-cased cleavage a Playboy model would envy.

Morgan forced herself to continue to smile. "Ashley, I'm pleased to meet you. Thanks for coming."

"My pleasure," Ashley cooed in reply. "Brad speaks so highly of you."

A nervous ripple fluttered through Morgan's gut as she considered what Brad might have said.

"Don't worry, it all can't be true." Vicki's voice popped up.

Morgan peeked at her sister. Vicki had a twinkle in her eyes and a smirk on her lips. Ashley flashed a surprised look at Vicki, then giggled softly before she placed her fingers to her lips.

Vicki turned to Brad. "We appreciate you coming."

Brad's expression darkened as he stared at Morgan's sister. Irritation flashed in his eyes. "Anything for a good cause," he added dryly.

Up until this afternoon Morgan hadn't realized Vicki wasn't a fan of Brad. Now she saw for the first time the feeling was mutual.

Brad turned back to her. "Morgan, any update on your stalker?" His eyes searched around behind her, lighting on Sabrina briefly. "Where's your bodyguard?"

"He's here," Morgan replied. "In fact, Sonoran Security has multiple people at the event tonight."

Brad glanced back to Morgan. The irritation from Vicki's comment had faded, and he looked worried. "I hope for your sake this ends soon, and no one gets hurt. Please take care."

Morgan's breath caught at his remark. She studied his expression. He appeared sincere and concerned for her safety, yet his words sounded like a threat. *I'm being paranoid.* "Thank you for your concern." She murmured.

"Well, we must find our seats," Brad said. He offered his arm to Ashley. The young blonde slid her arm through his and smiled at Morgan before he led her away from the line.

"God, I hate being right all the time," whispered Vicki as they moved out of earshot.

"Ashley seems nice," Morgan offered quietly.

"Yes, but he'll break her heart too."

"Perhaps."

"No, there is no perhaps or maybes about it. Morgan, Brad's a player. He led you along, and he'll do the same to her."

Morgan's eyes traveled across the room and found Shawn on the other side. He watched her. From the expression on his face, he'd figured out that Brad had arrived. He flashed a small smile and winked at her before he turned to work his way around the perimeter of the room, surveying the crowd.

***

So, the almighty lawyer ex-boyfriend finally arrived. The shock and confusion on Morgan's face had been a giveaway. Shawn pressed his lips together as he wondered why her ex had even bothered to show up. He would give his right eye tooth to have been closer and heard the conversation. He was proud of how quickly Morgan recovered and played the gracious hostess.

He tracked the lawyer and blonde as they located their seats. Shawn smirked as he watched the lawyer stroll from table to table before finding the place cards with their names on them. He'd seen the curvy blonde before. She was the one in the store trying on the ring and necklace the other day.

Part of Shawn wanted a quick man-to-man talk with Brad, to warn him. He had no love lost for opportunistic gold diggers. But the other part of him reveled in knowing this woman would play him, and Brad Marshall deserved it.

Shawn glanced back at Morgan who had settled back into the rhythm of greeting the guests. In the green evening gown, she stood out like an emerald in a sea of black ball gowns and dark suits. A flush of heat flickered through him as he remembered holding her in his arms. God, it had been so long since he felt this way about any woman and he'd tried to keep things on a professional level. Yet Morgan had gotten under his skin. A pause in the reception line gave her a moment's break. She glanced over at him, locked eyes and crooked a small smile. He grinned back. Oh Yeah. When this was over, this was going to get personal.

Shawn carefully studied the people at the tables. Guests settled into their chairs and chatted with each other. The wait staff came around adding water and bringing wine. On the far side, a tall young man with dark hair caught his attention. Dressed in a waiter's uniform, he moved tentatively to each table and poured water. The pitcher sloshed and water dribbled after he finished pouring each glass. *Rookie.* The young waiter looked up and scanned the room. His eyes settled on Shawn and their eyes locked for a few seconds before the young man looked away and returned to his duties.

Sabrina was doing an excellent job. Observant yet unobtrusive, she quietly shadowed Morgan while she worked the reception line and later visited the tables around the room. When the pair had returned from the salon earlier today he noticed Morgan had played fairy godmother. Sabrina's hair had been styled. Instead of the customary ponytail at the nape of her neck, the hair had been swept up into a riot of ebony curls which cascaded down to her shoulders.

In contrast, his afternoon hadn't been so luxurious. He examined the lists of the staff and guests and had investigated the hallways from the kitchen to the ballroom, noting possible routes of entry and exit.

His stomach growled in protest as the dinner service started. The food smelled fantastic, and he realized he hadn't eaten since lunch. *I should've grabbed something to eat earlier,* he thought as a server walked past him with a sizzling steak. The first thing he would do when this evening ended would be to order room service.

He located Morgan. She sat at a table filled with guests; her manner appeared relaxed as she conversed with the people around her. Her sister and parents were at separate tables. The seating was strategic. Each member of the family sat among prominent guests who were most likely to bid on the jewelry tonight.

Shawn had pulled a little strategic seating as well. Earlier this afternoon when he found Brad's name on the placement cards, he quietly moved them to place as much distance between them and Morgan as possible.

When he approached the last couple of tables he found Brad watching him with a cool, appraising expression. Shawn locked eyes with the man as he walked past the table. Neither man broke eye contact for several seconds. Then Brad looked away, turned to the guest on his left, and chatted.

Shawn stopped next to Sabrina who stood against the wall near Morgan's table. She peeked over at him. "Things are going well, you think?"

"Yes."

"So much for Morgan's stalker trying something," Sabrina said.

"Yeah, I'm beginning to wonder if he's given up."

"Do stalkers give up?"

Shawn hesitated before replying. Sabrina had a point. "No, most of the time they don't," he replied.

Sabrina shrugged. "Well, maybe this one doesn't like crowds."

"Hang in there, the evening will be over soon."

Sabrina nodded. Shawn left her, exited through the side door, and went back to the kitchen.

***

Morgan set her fork down beside her half-eaten steak. The silent showdown between Brad and Shawn gave her a bright moment in an otherwise emotionally uneven day. She glanced over her shoulder and found Sabrina standing alone against the wall. Shawn had been confident her stalker would make a move, but things had gone smoothly so far.

Her eyes scanned the room and couldn't find Shawn. Where is he? She tamped down the sense of aloneness and vulnerability that settled on her like a chill. She was being silly, not to mention clingy. There were up to two hundred people in the room. There was no way in the world that she was alone.

Morgan glanced across the centerpiece of pink roses and freesia. Could she and Shawn move forward after this whole mess was finished? Given a choice, she'd leave this table and seek him out, but she couldn't leave the high profile guests at it.

She glanced at her watch, only fifteen minutes away from the start of the auction bidding. After the jewelry had been sold, the night would wind down with music and dancing. Morgan then planned to slip away and retreat to her room to crash.

***

Shawn returned back to the ballroom in time to watch the auction. He hadn't checked the Internet auction in the past few hours, but the jewelry alone raised over one hundred fifty thousand dollars. If he factored the profit per plate on the dinner and the Internet monies, Shawn estimated the Kennedy family raised somewhere in the neighborhood of half a million dollars tonight.

The auction had been a fun playful affair with William standing at the front of the room, and his wife and daughters dashing around urging bidders and calling attention to the guests each time they placed a bid.

At one point, with the sapphire earrings up for bid, Morgan and Vicki had stood at opposite ends of the room and successfully promoted a straight up bidding war between two attendees. With each successive bid, the room got into the spirit of the contest, whooping and applauding.

Once the auction ended, the band returned and started their second set. Couples moved to the dance floor and Shawn scanned the room, searching for Morgan. He found her standing with her family, chatting with the couple who had purchased the diamond necklace.

She turned and locked eyes with him, her expression relaxed. The fundraiser, for all purposes, was over.

The band started a slow ballad, and the couples on the dance floor moved closer into each other's arms. Morgan continued to gaze at him, issuing an unspoken invitation.

He walked up to her and a small smile appeared on her lips. "Do you want to dance?"

"I'd love to."

She turned and, as she walked ahead of him to the dance floor, he reached out and touched the small of her back. "This event is an unqualified success," Shawn said.

Morgan looked up and smiled softly. "Yes, thank God. It's all downhill from now. All we need to do is lock the jewelry away, collect the proceeds and pay the bills. We won't start planning next year for a few months."

It's over. The phrase pinged through his mind. But it wasn't over. Morgan's stalker was still out there somewhere. Maybe this event had him a little spooked, but he hadn't given up and unless caught, he'd surface again.

On the dance floor, Morgan turned to him as he took her hand and gently slid his hand around her waist. She melted into his body in response. "Morgan, we need to have a talk tomorrow. We need to evaluate the situation with the stalker."

She sighed softly "I know. How about tomorrow morning? Eleven?"

"Fine."

"Hey Randall, over here," a man shouted. Morgan stiffened, and Shawn turned to where the voice came from. The bright light blinded him for a second followed by a laugh and another round of rapid flashes.

Morgan lurched back and raised her hand to shield her eyes. Shawn spun her around behind him and turned to face the man. The waiter from earlier this evening stood a few yards away and jeered. "Morgan, do you have a comment for Christy Thomas about you dating her former lover and the father of her daughter?"

"Damn." Shawn rushed the photographer and slapped the camera out of his hands. It crashed to the tile dance floor. "Hey, you're going to pay for that," the photographer screamed.

Shawn moved in close to grab the waiter, but the young man tried to escape by wiggling out of his waiter's jacket. Shawn released his grip, grabbed him by the collar of his shirt and slammed him down into the floor.

"Get off me. I'll sue you," the man yelled as he kicked and struggled. Shawn heard the collective gasp from the room and the muted buzz of conversation. He couldn't pick out specific comments, but he sure as hell knew what they must be saying.

Shawn bent the waiter's left arm behind his back which stopped his struggles. Shawn glanced up and saw Morgan's now pinched expression, a hand up over her mouth, her face pale.

Sabrina ran up to Shawn. "Get Morgan back to her room," Shawn growled. Sabrina nodded and went to Morgan. He glanced down at the photographer. "Okay, we can do this one of two ways.

If you play nice, I'll let you up and escort you out. If not..." Shawn leaned down and wrenched the man's arm tighter until he heard a grunt of protest. "Well?"

"Nice," The photographer hissed.

"Good choice."

Shawn stood up and backed up a step. As the man slowly stood up, Shawn grabbed the man by the arm, and walked him to the door. He glanced over at Brad as he passed his table. Morgan's ex-boyfriend cracked a small smile and nodded.

When they reached the ballroom entrance, Shawn shoved the door open and pushed the young man through it.

"I'm calling the police," The man whined. "You're gonna pay."

Shawn snorted. "No. I'm calling the police and before they arrive, you are going to answer some questions for me. Who are you and how did you find out about my daughter?"

***

"Morgan, let's go back to your room." Sabrina reached out and gently took her arm. Morgan surveyed the room. The remaining guests were murmuring and staring at the scene with rapt attention. Heat flushed her face. *Great, they think I'm the scarlet woman.* Morgan's stomach churned at what the fallout would be for Shawn and the fundraiser.

She glanced over at her parents, and Vicki strode across the room to her. Her sister forced a quick smile and locked her arm through Morgan's. "Let's go," she whispered.

Morgan straightened up. Her temples throbbed, and her eyes stung as she made her way through the crowd and out the door. They marched down the hall. On her right, the hotel security and

Shawn had the man off in the corner. By the look on Shawn's face the conversation had become ugly. Vicki tightened her hold and increased the pace as they virtually jogged past the group, heading to the lobby and elevators.

Her heart sank. Shawn must think she'd blabbed to someone about him and Christy. He'd told her if this info got out there'd be hell to pay. What would happen now? And how had that weasel found out about Shawn and Christy?

Once the elevators closed, her sister spoke, "That was a memorable finish to the evening. Care to talk about it?"

Morgan's throat went scratchy and her eyes stung as she blinked back tears. She brought her hands to her face, took a deep breath, and dropped them to her sides. "I wasn't supposed to talk to anyone about his daughter, Vicki, and I didn't."

"Well the cat's out of the bag now."

Morgan glanced over to her sister and shook her head. "A lot of harm could come from this."

She glanced over at Sabrina. The young security guard didn't look at her. "I wonder how that man found out," Sabrina whispered.

The elevator doors opened and they walked to Morgan's suite. Sabrina checked the rooms first. When the all clear was given, Morgan and Vicki entered, locking the door behind them.

Morgan shot a glance over at Sabrina. "I didn't say anything. Honestly, I didn't. Why would I? I've only known about this for a little over forty-eight hours. I don't have any contacts in the entertainment industry. And thanks to that idiot downstairs, people think I'm a home-wrecker. The fundraiser has a lot to lose with negative publicity like this, even the store. For me to say something to the press makes absolutely no sense."

"You never mentioned it to me," Vicki said.

Sabrina looked at Morgan and nodded. "Give Shawn time. He'll get an answer."

"From his reaction, I'll bet he'll get to the bottom of it tonight," Vicki said.

Her sister glanced over at Morgan. "The best thing that you can do is try to get a good night's sleep. There's nothing you can do. Let Shawn sort it out."

Morgan nodded. "You're right. I don't know how I'm going to sleep, but you're right."

"Well, I'm ordering room service first," Sabrina said.

"I'll see you tomorrow at breakfast with mom and dad," Vicki said.

Morgan glanced at her sister. What are her parents thinking right now? Vicki threw her a knowing glance. "Relax. The event was a success despite what happened. You did a great job."

Her sister walked forward and gave Morgan a hug. "It'll be okay."

Morgan exhaled. "I hope you're right."

Vicki pulled back. "Let's see what Shawn finds out." The younger woman reached over and picked up her evening clutch. "Get some sleep."

Sabrina locked the door after Vicki left. Morgan returned to her bedroom and shut the door. She tossed her purse on the bed and slipped out of her heels. As she replayed the event in her mind, she gritted her teeth. When it first happened she thought her stalker had shown up. Where was he now?

***

Shawn decided to make a final check in with Sabrina. Then go to his room to order dinner and get a hot shower. The police arrived, and after some negotiation, the young man had decided to leave and not press charges for assault in exchange for not being charged for trespassing and stalking.

The guy had been a rank amateur. The paparazzi-wannabe infiltrated the event by stealing a uniform and working as wait staff. When the opportunity to get a picture of Morgan and Shawn together turned up, he went for the money shot. After some discussion, the photographer admitted that his source had been an ex-employee of Christy's.

Deep in his heart, he knew that Emma's paternity couldn't be kept secret forever, but the fact that the leak came from Christy's side gave him a measure of relief. There wasn't a lot Christy and her team of lawyers could do to him about this. But Christy's ex-housekeeper was going to find herself in a world of hurt very quickly. Shawn's former girlfriend was not the type to let a breach of a confidentiality agreement slide by.

As the adrenaline evaporated, Shawn felt like his legs were made of rubber as he made his way back to Morgan's hotel room. This week had been a real marathon. He'd done bodyguard work before, but you did a shift of eight hours and then someone else took over. This had been a twenty-four seven experience, and he needed a rest. A small smile crossed his face, not that guarding Morgan had been all bad.

His phone buzzed in his jacket pocket. He retrieved it and frowned. *Who would be calling at this hour?* He picked up the call. "Hello?"

"Shawn Randall?" the masculine voice on the line asked.

"Speaking."

"Mr. Randall, my name is Detective Cole. I'm calling to advise you we have a match on the fingerprints from Morgan's car."

Shawn stopped. Finally, they were going to get a break in this case. "Who is he?"

"His name is Frank Kaufman. He's twenty years old and lives on the West side. He has a record for stalking and assault."

"Stalking and assault? You mean he's done this before?"

"About a year ago. He's currently on probation. We sent over a squad car to pick him up for questioning. Hold please."

Shawn continued to walk down the hall while he held the line. The best news would be if the detective reported they had him in custody. "Mr. Randall?"

"Yes. The officers who went to Kaufman's house report that he's not there. His grandmother reported that Frank is at work tonight."

"Where does he work?"

"Copper Creek Inn."

Shawn froze. "Say again?"

"He's working tonight at Copper Creek Inn."

"Send squad cars over here now," Shawn ordered before he flipped the cell phone closed and broke into a dead run.

CHAPTER 18

Frank stood by the room service cart laden with food and a bottle of champagne. He was being checked out, and he knew it. A few moments delay after he knocked on the door didn't alarm him; everybody looked out the security peephole before they let him in. He adjusted the champagne bottle which laid in the ice bucket. His hands had a slight nervous tremor. Now what he'd dreamed about and planned for was about to happen. Within seconds he'd be with Morgan. All he had to do was hold it together a little longer. The door opened and a petite woman with dark hair studied him.

"Room service," he said.

She stepped aside, and he entered pushing the cart ahead of him. He scanned the room discretely, looking for Morgan. His heart pounded rapidly, and he struggled to breathe normally.

"Put the food over here," the woman directed.

Frank moved the cart to where she requested and gave quick verbal check off of the items on the cart. The dark-haired lady nodded as he went over the order until he pointed out the champagne bottle in the ice bucket.

"I didn't order that."

"Compliments of the house," he replied.

The puzzled look on her face told him she seemed to doubt his answer but replied, "Okay. Thanks."

"Please sign here," Frank requested as he handed over the room service receipt.

The lady took the invoice from him, "Do you have a pen?"

Frank patted his jacket pocket in an attempt to locate one. He hoped she bought the act. "Sorry, I thought I had one on me."

"Wait a sec." She turned and walked over to the desk in the corner.

Now. Frank reached down, slid the champagne bottle out of the ice bucket and crept up behind her. Just as she pulled the pen out of the desk drawer, he raised the bottle up and slammed it on the woman's head. She fell to the floor in a heap.

For a brief moment, Frank stared at her on the carpet in disbelief. Is she really unconscious? He gently nudged the woman's body with his foot. When she didn't move he set the bottle down and turned to search for Morgan.

The bedroom door on the right was closed. He walked over, almost tiptoeing, and laid his head against it. Someone had the TV on so he knocked softly.

The door opened. "Sabrina?" Morgan paused. For a few seconds, they were face-to-face and he stood speechless drinking in the moment. "Where's Sabrina?" she asked.

Frank froze. He had planned this meeting for weeks. He dreamed and practiced a million things to say. But he never thought about how to answer the simple question she posed.

Morgan glanced past him and spied the woman on the floor. The flow of emotions on her face fascinated him as they ran across her in slow motion.

Her eyes rolled from Sabrina to him, and she paled as the pieces fell into place. "Dear God! No!" Morgan gasped as she stepped back and tried to slam the door in his face. Frank raised his hands to push back to stop her. Morgan leaned in, and he shouldered his whole weight against the wooden door.

The door flew open and Frank tumbled into the room falling face first on the carpet. Flashes of light preceded a loud crack. His cheek burned like fire as he skidded across the floor. Dazed, he raised his head and searched for Morgan. Tears blinded his vision and the searing pain from his nose and the copper taste on his lips meant his nose was bleeding and broken. His tears cleared and he spied Morgan rolling off her back, scrambling to her feet.

"Get away from me," Morgan screamed as she dashed for the door.

He lunged for her and caught her by the ankle. Her strong pull on his arm spun him around, and as she hit the ground for a second time he scrambled over to grab her.

He gasped raggedly. "Morgan, stop. I won't hurt you."

She rolled around and fired off a hard kick at him, and then another trying to free herself from his grasp.

"Quit it," he yelled as concern gave way to anger. He didn't think Morgan would try to hurt him or escape.

Desperately hanging onto her ankle, Frank sat up, leaned back and gave a violent jerk causing her to slide closer to him.

She screamed and tried to roll to her side to get to her feet. Frank pounced and landed on top of her.

She would do what he wanted now.

***

Shawn's lungs burned as he took the stairs two at a time and reached the landing in the stairwell on Morgan's floor. He had to make sure she was safe. The police were on the way, but he was closer. Where was the sick son-of-a-bitch? The best outcome would be that they were safe and sound behind a locked hotel room door. *Please God, let that be the case.*

He pulled open the heavy metal door and sprinted down the hallway. The hotel room doors flowed in a blur and as he neared her room the door stood wide open.

He halted and pulled his pistol out of the holster before he hugged the wall. He angled himself to get maximum visibility as he peered inside. Over to the right, a cart with food sat undisturbed. He rolled to the other side of the entrance, scanned the other half of the room and found Sabrina on the floor.

"Damn!" He stepped into the room scanning left and right. The place appeared empty and he raced over to Sabrina. Shawn crouched down. "Sabrina?"

No response. She appeared to be breathing normally, but he needed to get her medical help and fast. Shawn stood up and turned to Morgan's bedroom.

"Morgan!"

She emerged in the doorway pale and silent. It took a couple seconds to register, but Frank stood behind her with his arm around her neck and a knife to her throat.

Shawn instantly raised his gun.

They stopped.

"Don't," the man behind her ordered.

Shawn couldn't fire. He didn't have a clean shot. But he wouldn't let his arm drop, so they stood for a few seconds sizing each other up.

Morgan had a dazed expression on her face. She had been hit, and her left cheek was red and looked to be swelling up. For what it was worth, her stalker looked worse. Blood streamed from his nose and chin, dripping onto Morgan.

Frank spoke first. "Get out of our way."

His voice was deep and calm. Shawn hoped maybe he might talk their way out of this.

"No. I can't do that. Frank, we need to talk."

The man blinked. "You know who I am?"

"Yeah, I do. So do the police. They matched your fingerprints to one of the prints on Morgan's car."

"Police," the young man growled. He took a deep breath, then shuddered when he exhaled. Then a determined gleam appeared in his eyes. "Move, we're getting out of here. Together."

This time, the tone of Frank's voice had changed. An edgy nervous quality had replaced the calmness from a few seconds ago. *He's going to lose it*, Shawn thought.

Frank tightened his hold on Morgan, pressing the blade firmly against her neck. Her eyes widened in terror as her shock melted away. "She's mine. Not yours. I won't leave without her."

To bring the point home he pressed the knife deeper into Morgan's neck and a small crimson trickle slid down the blade.

"Easy! Easy! Let's talk this out. Frank, you're drawing blood. You're hurting her."

Frank blinked. He softened the pressure against her neck. "I don't want to hurt her. I never wanted to hurt her. I love her," he uttered.

Shawn waited and tried to figure what to say next. Sabrina moaned and Frank glanced over at her before tightening the knife against Morgan's throat. "We have to go, now. Drop the gun and back away."

Shawn weighed the options. The police were coming which meant Frank wouldn't get far if he got past him. If he held them here, the situation would harden into a hardcore hostage standoff with Morgan on the wrong side of it. Her stalker was barely rational. The odds of her getting hurt increased exponentially if they became trapped.

"Okay," Shawn replied. "I'm setting my pistol down. See?"

Shawn slowly set the pistol on the floor, then stood up and stepped back. Shawn stared over at Morgan and his chest tightened. He'd failed her. "I'm sorry," he said softly. She stared back in silence. He read her face. The terror of a few seconds ago had melted and she appeared to be planning something. He could see her working something out, but what?

"Move up," Frank ordered and nudged Morgan forward to the gun. When they reached the place Shawn set his weapon down, Frank ordered Morgan to crouch down with him so he could pick it up. He almost succeeded when without warning Morgan pushed backwards, tumbling on Frank, and pinning him to the floor.

Fearing that he would lose her, Frank abandoned trying to reach the gun but before he could get a firm grip on Morgan, she sank her teeth into his arm.

Frank screamed and Shawn charged, peeling Frank's arm away from her.

"Run," Shawn shouted as he broke the stalker's hold on her. Morgan scrambled out of reach but Shawn felt Frank's weight shift.

"He's going for the gun," Morgan shouted.

"You ruined it," the deranged man screamed as he writhed and lurched for the weapon. Shawn crashed down on top of the stalker and lunged for Frank's arm to prevent him from grasping his gun, but he was too late. The younger man clutched the weapon and tried to point it at Shawn.

The handgun's muzzle waved all over the place as the two men wrestled. It discharged and the recoil ricocheted down both men's arms. A second shot sent blinding pain into Shawn's leg. His body tightened, and he reached down to his thigh. His head slammed into the carpet as his head rolled to the side. Morgan scrambled over to him.

"Get away from him!" Frank shouted.

"No!" Morgan yelled.

Shawn glanced up. Frank had the gun and leveled the muzzle at the couple.

"We're going." Frank growled. He edged around them and moved to the door. As he reached down to grab Morgan, she wrenched her arm out of his hold. Suddenly Frank's face took on a shocked, wounded expression, before he fell to the carpet. The young man convulsed for a few seconds and then was still.

Within seconds, he recovered and tried to stand up when another group of seizures followed. A crackling noise filled the air.

Shawn rolled his head around and found Sabrina with the Tazer in her hands.

"Grab the gun," Sabrina ordered. When the electric current stopped, Morgan scrambled over and yanked the gun out of Frank's hand. Frank moaned and tried to get up for a third time but Sabrina nailed him again.

"Atta girl, fry the son-of-a-bitch," Shawn growled.

Sabrina staggered over and took the gun from Morgan and held it on Frank. "Morgan, call the police," she ordered.

Shawn grasped his leg and sank back on the carpet. "They're on their way," he groaned. "Call for an ambulance."

Morgan scrambled over to the phone, and Shawn glanced over at Sabrina who continued to hold the gun on Morgan's stalker. The young woman appeared dazed. She slowly swayed back and forth as she balanced on her feet. "Morgan, make that two ambulances," Shawn added.

Morgan returned to him and glanced down at his leg. "Oh My God," she whispered. She spun and dashed to the bathroom and returned with every towel she could bring. She unfolded a clean towel and applied pressure to his leg.

Shawn stiffened and hissed as the throbbing pain went nuclear. Morgan glanced up at him and he read dry-eyed, sober concern in her eyes.

"So much blood," Morgan murmured as she leaned down heavily on his wound.

Shawn looked down at her hands, and weakness washed over him. It looked bad.

"Lay down." Morgan ordered. Shawn complied, and she lifted his leg and stuffed pillows and towels under it to elevate his thigh. He grimaced and hissed.

Morgan looked at his face. "Sorry. Sorry."

The vibration of running feet thumped through his shoulders and back. "I think the police are here." He smiled, exhaled, and closed his eyes.

CHAPTER 19

Morgan stormed through the glass doors in the emergency entrance so quickly she barely cleared them as they opened.

"Morgan, over here," Vicki said.

Her head snapped in the direction of the voice and found her sister standing off to the side waiting for her. She looked calm, but her eyes held a worried air.

"I got here as soon as I could. How's Shawn?"

Vicki extended her arms wide open, and Morgan moved in and hugged her. "He's in surgery. We hope to know something soon," she whispered.

Morgan gulped and she pulled back to gaze in her sister's face. "The police report took so long. God, Vic, there was so much blood."

Vicki nodded. Morgan's eyes watered for what must've been the hundredth time since the attack and her knees behaved like they were made of Jell-O.

Her sister tightened her grip. "Come on. Don't lose it now." Vicki grasped Morgan's arms, "Breathe."

Morgan inhaled deeply and exhaled slowly. Her sister gave her a small smile. "Good, again."

Morgan drew another breath but before she finished exhaling, the younger sister swung her around and marched her down the hallway. As they reached the elevator, Vicki punched the button and Morgan stared blindly at the metallic door.

"Get ready. There's quite a crowd in the waiting room."

Morgan cast a glance at her. "I can imagine."

"Yeah, Mom, Dad, Sabrina's family, and Matt are upstairs." The door opened, and the two women stepped in. "You missed the explosion."

Morgan arched her brow, "What explosion?"

Vicki chuckled. "Sabrina struck me as a quiet person, but she can put up quite a fight when you try to make her do something she doesn't want to do. Like spend the night under observation in the hospital."

"Is she still here?" Morgan asked.

Vick grinned. "Matt arrived and put his foot down. He said if she walked out of the hospital tonight, he'd fire her."

"I'm sure that went over well." Morgan wrapped her arms around herself and began to rub them. "Why are hospitals so cold?"

"Between you and me I think Sabrina has a bit of a crush on Matt," Vicki added.

The elevator door opened and Vicki led her down the hall to the waiting room. As Morgan rounded the corner, she found her parents huddled with another couple and a young teen-aged boy.

William Kennedy stood up with her mother, and the couple walked over and hugged her. Morgan clung to her mother, took deep breaths, and closed her eyes to banish the tears that welled up. Then she opened her eyes and sought out Matt. He stood off to the side of the room, away from the families and leaned against a credenza. She studied his face in an effort to read what might be happening. His lips were pressed together firmly, and his relaxed posture didn't hide the worry in his eyes.

Morgan looked away. It must be bad. She pulled back from her mother's arms. "How long has Shawn been in surgery?"

Her mother glanced at her wrist watch. "About two hours."

"He could have died tonight."

"But he won't," her sister responded.

William spoke. "Morgan, it's over. Your stalker is in police custody."

Morgan nodded. "Yes. Did you know he stalked someone else about a year ago?"

"How could this happen?" Morgan's mother asked.

"He slipped through the system, I guess. He needs serious psychological help. Maybe this time he'll get it," Morgan answered.

The older woman shook her head, and anger flashed in her eyes. "How do you slip through the system?"

"Elaine. Relax." William said as he touched his wife's arm. "He'll never get a chance to do this again."

Morgan glanced back at Matt. He watched the family with a cool, detached expression. "Mom, dad, have you met Shawn's business partner, Matt?"

"Yes. He's very nice, dear."

"Speaking of meeting people," William Kennedy interrupted. "Let me introduce you to Sabrina's family." Her father gently took her by the arm and walked her over to the couple and a teenage boy sitting quietly. "Morgan, this is Benito and Margarita Diaz. They're Sabrina's parents, and this handsome young man is her brother, Roberto."

The older man stood and extended his hand. "A pleasure to meet you." His polite demeanor failed to hide the tired worried look in his espresso-colored eyes.

"Sabrina was very brave tonight," Morgan said. "She actually took my stalker down. You should be proud of her."

A frown popped up on the man face. "Proud? Yes. I'm proud of my daughter. But I don't think she should be putting herself in such dangerous circumstances. She must leave this job. I will insist."

Morgan pressed her lips together firmly as she shook his hand. What would Sabrina do after today? She clearly loved her job and yet her parents were against her continuing in this position. "My sister said she is staying tonight for observation."

"Yes. We've all insisted after hearing what the doctor's said. My daughter has a strong will." Benito took a breath and paused. He appeared to want to say more but chose instead to keep his thoughts private. He smiled. "This is my wife, Margarita."

Morgan turned and extended a hand only to be warmly hugged from the petite woman. "I'm glad you're here. It's like we're family," Sabrina's mother whispered as she patted Morgan's shoulder.

Guilt pinged through Morgan, and she squeezed the middle-aged woman. "I tried to get here as soon as I could. The police insisted I stay and give a full report on what happened."

"Hush," the woman replied as she pulled back and looked Morgan in the face. "We know."

Morgan glanced over at Matt and found him watching the exchange. *Why is he sitting off by himself?* She detected a fleeting change of expression from a few minutes ago. The concern in his eyes had melted into what she could only interpret as longing before he turned and stared at the television screen.

Morgan shifted her attention back to Benito and Margarita and chatted with them for a few minutes before sinking into the chair beside her parents. She rubbed her forehead as she fought off the physical exhaustion which slithered through her limbs and sucked the energy from her. Shawn had been in surgery for two hours and they'd not heard anything. Every time someone in scrubs traveled down the hallway past the waiting area, Morgan would lock onto them and pray they were coming over to give everyone news.

Finally, Morgan stood up and walked over to Matt. The lean sandy-haired Texan regarded her approach, but made no comment.

"Matt?"

"Not now," he said.

She stopped. Was he angry with her about what happened? She opened her mouth to speak, but no words came.

"Go sit before you fall down," he said. Exhaustion threaded through his quiet voice.

"We need to talk." Morgan said.

Matt nodded. "I know. We will, but not now."

Morgan took a slow deep breath and turned to sit down next to her sister. She leaned back in the chair and stared at the TV mounted on the wall. The cable news show talked about the upcoming election, but Morgan couldn't focus. The events of the day replayed over and over in her head.

Finally, a gray-haired man in surgical scrubs arrived, "Matt Anderson?"

Morgan leaned up in her seat. She could feel everyone around her tense but she stayed seated as Matt approached the doctor. They spoke for a few minutes. Her mouth felt like she'd been sucking on cotton. Matt shook the doctor's hand and walked to the families. He flashed a weary smile. "He's going to be all right."

Relief washed through her. As she tried to stand, her knees buckled and she sank back into the chair cushion.

"He's in recovery right now and should be there for a while. They don't expect to move him to a room for a few hours yet. I would suggest everyone go home and try to get some sleep." Matt added.

"Good idea," William Kennedy said. He turned, stood up, and waited as his wife picked up her purse and water bottle.

"Morgan, are you coming?" Elaine asked.

"Hmm?"

"Do you want us to walk you to your car?" Her father asked.

"No. I'm going to stay a bit longer." Morgan cast a glance over at Matt.

"Honey, Shawn won't be ready to see visitors until tomorrow afternoon. Maybe you should go home and come back when he's awake."

Morgan shook her head. "No. I'm staying. I'll give you a call tomorrow." She glanced down at her wrist watch. "Correction, later today."

Her mother nodded and her parents started walking down the hall after the Diaz family.

"Are you sure you don't want me to keep you company?" Vicki asked.

Morgan smiled. "No. I'm fine. Go back to the hotel and get some sleep."

After the families left, Morgan turned and found Matt staring at her. He crooked a small tired grin. "Let the receptionist know why you're here and they'll update you when they move him to a private room."

Morgan nodded. "Will do."

Shawn's partner reached out and gave her arm a gentle squeeze before he ambled down the hall.

Morgan checked in with the nurse's station and sank back into the chair. The empty seating area and the cold air-conditioning contributed to a sense of numbness that chilled her body and mind.

Shawn's going to be okay. She wrapped her arms across her body and rubbed them with her palms. My God, there'd had been so much blood. She feared he might have bled to death before the paramedics and the ambulance arrived. As if her body were reliving the ordeal, an adrenaline jolt coursed through her. Jumpy, she stood up and ambled over to the window to look at the twinkling lights on the horizon as the sky lightened to a dusky purple.

What would happen next? Morgan bit her lip and took a deep breath. The past few days had been a nightmare and the only thing that had made it bearable, no, survivable, had been Shawn. Would their budding relationship survive this?

She exhaled slowly. Life came with no guarantees. She understood that now. Strange how an event triggers many others, like threads woven in fabric.

Samuel died accidentally. Her family's passion to make his death serve good gave birth to a fundraiser, which had bloomed beyond everyone's expectations. Morgan swallowed and her lip trembled when she remembered how she placed her dreams of becoming a jewelry designer on the back shelf to run things after her father's heart attack. Then her break-up with Brad, the stalker, and now the arrival of a man who showed her again how fragile and vulnerable life can be.

Morgan dropped her arms and stretched as she slowly rolled her neck from side to side. Things would have to change from this point forward. She'd continue managing the fundraiser, but her father must hire someone to manage the store so that she could focus on her jewelry designing. Brad? He'd moved on and now she would too. The mountains in the distance were outlined in an aura of sunlight and the horizon took on an orange glow.

"Miss Kennedy?"

Morgan turned to the nurse who had walked up behind her. "Yes?"

"They're moving him. Come to the counter. I'll give you his room number and directions on how to get there."

"Thank you."

Morgan arrived just after they moved him from the gurney to the bed. She walked over and touched his arm. Shawn rolled his head over and smiled when he saw her. "I'm fine," he murmured before his eyes closed. His voice had a fuzzy, sleepy quality about it. The nurse came in and adjusted the IV. "He's going to be out for a few more hours. You won't be missing much if you want to go home."

"Can I stay?" She pointed to the recliner on the side of the bed. "I won't be in anyone's way. Please."

The nurse evaluated her and commented, "I think you better sit before you fall down. Let me get you a blanket."

***

Shawn thought he heard Jerry Springer. His closed eyes registered a dim light and he slowly opened them to a TV and yes, the Jerry Springer Show was on. He stared at the screen as a cheating husband went public about his infidelity to a shocked, angry wife and in front of the whole world. The studio audience jeered him, cheered his wife, and geared up for a smack down between the wife and lover. Shawn began to fumble for the remote. He'd had enough of smack downs for a while. Anything, even Dr. Phil, would be preferable to this.

Shawn rolled his head to the side and found Morgan sprawled on the recliner fast asleep. Reaching over, he touched her hand that spilled over the armrest and her eyes sprang open.

"Hi," he whispered.

Morgan kicked the blanket back, climbed out of the chair, and stood at the side of his bed. "Welcome back."

She caressed his arm carefully to avoid where the IV needle was taped down. "How do you feel?"

"Not bad. What happened after I left?"

Morgan smiled. "Frank Kaufman is in custody, and Sabrina's in the hospital for observation. Don't worry. Just rest and focus on recovering."

"Good," Shawn said.

"It's more than good," a low masculine voice responded. Shawn glanced over to where Matt stood at the door. "Frank's been charged with stalking, assault, attempted murder, not to mention the obvious probation violation issue. I think I can safely predict when he gets arraigned he won't be able to make bail."

"You never know the kinds of deals that can be struck when the lawyers get involved," Shawn replied.

"No negotiated deals this time," Matt replied. "I had an off-the-record conversation and found out Brad's firm handled Frank's case the last time. This time, there'll be no plea bargain."

Shawn cursed. "Brad knew."

Matt shrugged. "Maybe, even if he did, Brad couldn't say anything about it: attorney/client privilege."

Shawn began to fidget in bed. "His silence could have gotten us killed."

Morgan gently laid her hand on his shoulder and interrupted, "Shawn, relax and don't move your leg around. You could make things worse."

Shawn took a deep breath, "I'll deal with him later."

"Later is good," Morgan replied. Her voice held an amused quality to it as if a small laugh simmered below the surface.

The doctor came in the room. "Mr. Randall, your surgery went well, and your vitals are good. I'd like to keep you a couple more days and then we'll release you to go home. I want you to keep the leg elevated for the next few days, and you'll be on crutches for a while. Do you have support at home for a few days?"

Shawn paused. Morgan would be exiting his life. She didn't need him anymore. "No, but I can…"

"He's coming home to stay with me," Morgan said.

Shawn rolled his head to stare at her. "You don't have to…" but he never had a chance to finish his sentence. Morgan leaned over and planted a kiss on him.

She pulled back and gently caressed his face, "I won't take no for an answer."

Shawn slid his hand up to her face and pulled her down for another kiss. Only after hearing Matt clearing his throat did the couple stop and look at him.

"Well, I'm glad that's settled," Matt drawled.

EPILOGUE

Two weeks later –

Morgan pretended to ignore Shawn as he bounced his uninjured leg on the ball of his foot. She smiled. Emma arrived today, and he was as excited as a child on Christmas morning waiting to open his presents.

Upon his discharge from the hospital, Morgan moved Shawn into her guest bedroom, spent the next few days caring for him and sketching designs on her dining room table. Within a week, she was back at the store, wrapping up the final details from the fundraiser.

Even Shawn returned to the office for a few hours each day and worked on paperwork. Now he'd started putting weight on the leg for short periods of time and moved about reasonably well, even abandoning the crutches for short periods. When at home they talked and planned for Emma's arrival.

As Morgan pulled off the fifty-one parkway's exit ramp into Sky Harbor airport, she took a deep breath and exhaled. Her stomach fluttered. A few days back, she had spoken to Emma for the first time on the phone. She seemed a sweet child, but still a part of her wasn't certain what she would encounter today.

"I'll drop you off at the arrival side of the terminal and park the car. Do you want to wait for me at the ticket counter or should I meet you at the security gate?"

"I'll wait for you at the ticket counter." Shawn said.

"You've got it."

Within minutes she pulled up on the north side of terminal four and waited as he slid out and pulled out his crutches. Morgan smiled as he made his way through the sliding glass doors to the terminal. The cool no-nonsense man she met a few weeks ago was the complete opposite of the loving engaged man in her life now.

She found him in front of the ticket counter leaning on his crutches. "The plane's on time. Joan, her au pair, will be with her when Emma gets off the plane, but she'll take a return flight within a couple hours once she drops Emma off."

Morgan nodded. "Ready?"

Shawn flashed a grin. "Yeah."

The couple walked to the elevators. Then made their way to the security gates and waited as wave after wave of passengers filed past them. Morgan scoured the crowds wondering how different Emma might look from the photos in Shawn's office.

"There." Shawn pointed to a middle-aged woman and a young girl dressed in jeans and a light pink top.

"There's my girl." His voice radiated with pride and affection.

Morgan studied the young girl. It wasn't hard to miss the re-semblance. In addition to her father's crystal blue eyes she had his crooked grin and when it broke into a full smile it showcased a missing front tooth.

Emma spied him and dashed the remaining few yards into her father's open arms. As she neared him, he dropped his crutches and bent down to scoop her up.

Morgan stood back, giving the pair their space.

"Mommy said you were hurt," Emma said.

"I'm okay now," Shawn replied. He turned to Morgan as he set his daughter down on her feet. Morgan took a shallow breath and held it. *What had Christy said about her?*

"Emma, I'd like you to meet someone very special. This is Morgan."

Morgan flashed a smile despite her uncertainty and extended her hand, "Hi Emma. I'm so glad to meet you."

The child broke into the grin Morgan loved to see in her father. Then, without a word, she ran over and gave Morgan a big hug.

Thank you for reading Someone to Watch Over Me. I hope you enjoyed this book and would be interested in helping other readers find out about it through one of the following methods:

Please feel free to share it with a friend if the version you've purchased is lending enabled.

Recommend it to friends and fellow readers.

Leave a review. Inform other readers why you.

If you do write a review, please send me an email at taylor-michaelsauthor@gmail.com. I'll gift you a digital copy of the next book as a way of thanking you.

Coming Fall-Winter

PLAYING WITH FIRE
By Taylor Michaels

When Stella Adams leaves her family's construction business, her decision angers her father and alienates her from the rest of her family. Determined to prove her family wrong about her ability to successfully remodel and sell homes, she prepares to go it alone. When Matt Anderson arrives on the construction site, she knows the only possible reason for his appearance is that her father sent him.

Matt Anderson disappeared from college one night ten years ago and started a whole new life. Estranged from his family, he fiercely guards the reason why he left. Now a successful wealthy businessman, he's comfortable keeping the world at arm's length. When Stella's father approaches Matt about getting Stella to hire his firm for construction site security, he finds himself drawn into a family battle where he's an unlikely peacemaker.

After Matt discovers a rash of house fires in the area and a string of construction site accidents, he must convince Stella that she genuinely needs his company's services. But there's a bigger problem, he's falling for the strong-willed home remodeler. How can he reconcile Stella with her family when he can't find the courage to go home himself?

CPSIA information can be obtained
at www.ICGtesting.com
Printed in the USA
LVHW08s1622141018
593523LV00012B/285/P

9 781480 146754